ORPHAN JIM

ORPHAN JIM

JIM

A NOVEL

Lonnie Coleman

DOUBLEDAY & COMPANY, INC.
GARDEN CITY, NEW YORK
1975

All of the characters in this book are fictitious, and any resemblance to actual persons, living or dead, is purely coincidental.

ISBN: 0-385-11085-5
LIBRARY OF CONGRESS CATALOG CARD NUMBER 75-7253
Copyright © 1975 by Lonnie Coleman
ALL RIGHTS RESERVED
PRINTED IN THE UNITED STATES OF AMERICA
FIRST EDITION

To *James Oliver Brown*

Happy days are here again . . .
Popular song of the Depression

A day! Help! Help! Another day!
Emily Dickinson

ORPHAN JIM

CHAPTER 1

Nineteen thirty-two is a long time ago, and the farm where we lived is a long way away. As the years accumulate around me, much is lost to memory, or deliberately set aside, but that time and place grow like a hill that only begins to show its size the farther away from it I go.

I was thirteen. There are no pictures of me, but I must have been an ugly girl. I was runty and built straight up and down: front, back, and sides. I had thick brown hair that never had been cut by anybody but me or Mama, and then just sawed off with dull sewing scissors.

My brother Jim was seven, and Mama had spoiled him,

letting him stay a baby as much as it lay in her power to do. Out of her sight I pinched and sometimes pushed and even hit him, not so much to hurt him as to let him know there was such a one as me in this world. I did not like him, but at least he didn't squawl when I touched him. Mama hadn't let him go to school when he turned six but taught him herself, what letters and numbers were for, and how to read a little. I could remember when Mama was pretty, but Jim couldn't; he was too young. She was so wasted away it hurt to look at her by the time the Lord took her in May 1932.

When that happened, Jim was lost; he couldn't take it in. He'd sit on the floor looking at the chair where she'd spent most of her time, like she'd gone out of the room for a minute and would be right back.

Papa slunk around feeling sorry for himself and not doing any work. Not that there was much to do, for he hadn't bothered to put in a crop back in the spring, when Mama looked to go from one day to the next. I fed the mule with what I could find growing wild he'd eat and we couldn't. There were a few scrawny chickens that mostly scratched their own living out of the ground. Papa had sold the cow to buy Mama's coffin. We'd killed the last two hogs way-gone in January. The lard was used up except for a smear and a scrape but if I put my face in the tin tub that had held it, my stomach gripped with pork hunger.

It was hard times right enough. I didn't know enough to call it "the Depression" as everybody did later, although I'd gone to school regular, even with Mama sick and all. The house had never been anything, three rooms, one with a fireplace. There was a well with a rope so old we didn't risk drawing a full bucket of water at one time. No road led to us, just wagon tracks with weeds growing thick and tall down the middle; a car had to go fast to get over them without stalling.

Mr. Petrie, who owned our farm, came a few times after Mama died to look around, but Papa was never there. For a while he suspected Papa of hiding from him, but then he believed me. The last time Mr. Petrie came I stood in the door and watched him. He shook his head all the way back from the barn and said to me: "I don't like to dog a man that's had bad trouble, but your Pa has let the summer run through his fingers without trying to make up his losses. You tell him I was here and sure didn't like what I saw."

"Yes, sir."

"You tell him to come see me, and I don't mean maybe." He walked toward his old Ford, then turned like he wasn't satisfied he'd said enough. "You all have got to get off my place before winter. I won't have your Pa here doing nothing."

I didn't answer. There didn't seem to be any more to say, and after fussing to himself over the steering wheel, he backed out over the wagon tracks.

I'd long had the idea, but I vowed then to do it. Go. Not with Papa, not with Jim. I didn't want anybody to worry about but me, myself, and I.

Of course, I didn't let on to Papa when he came home other than to tell him what Mr. Petrie had said. Papa almost always came home, but real late, when Jim had gone to bed. He'd appear with his shirttail out, face smeared with dirt or blood, mouth open like he was trying to laugh or had gone half crazy. Sometimes he'd cry and wake Jim up and try to love us, hug us; but that just scared Jim and disgusted me, smelling as Papa did of liquor and sweat and puke. Then he'd say nobody loved him, and it was a fact: nobody did.

3

One day a black dog came trotting up the wagon tracks, stopped in the yard under our one chinaberry tree, and lifted his head to sniff for food. Jim happened to be standing there like a statue doing nothing, and the dog made friends with him. I was so surprised at Jim's showing interest in anything I didn't make an objection when he took the dog around the house to the kitchen door and fed him. There was only corn bread I'd cooked for noon dinner but Jim hadn't touched and I'd thought we'd save for supper.

In no time he'd named the dog Smut and they were thick as seeds in a sunflower. Smut didn't make up to me any. When I cooked for us that evening he could tell I wasn't going to offer him anything. Jim gave him half the peas and corn bread on his plate. That dog thought of nothing but a full gut. I was glad when a week later he sniffed off after a skinny old hound bitch with flies clouding around her butt. Let them drift, I thought, and beg somebody else's scraps.

But Jim was just distracted. He went hither and yonder calling Smut's name and whistling for him, but Smut didn't come. He said to me that evening, "You reckon old Smut will come home after he gets tired of doing it?"

That was the first I knew of Jim's understanding such matters. He must have picked it up from some boys at Sunday School. Mama had made both of us go, although we had to walk a mile to and from town. I didn't answer him.

"Trudy, you don't *care* if my dog never comes home!" he accused.

"No, I don't," I said, and gave him a little push. "Go wash your feet before supper."

CHAPTER 2

Every town has at least one self-elected Right Hand of the Lord. Pluma's was a fat woman with a nest of brown warts on one side of her neck, two ugly grown daughters, and a husband who spent all his time making medicines at the back of the drugstore her father had left them when he died.

Mrs. Rice had time over from family concerns to help others. She bossed the Sunday School and had considerable say-so in the Monday-to-Friday school. She visited the sick with Bible pictures she ordered from Birmingham, and gave warnings of destruction to the town drunkards that hung around the train depot. She urged the weak to get some starch into their souls; and she mourned with those who suffered the loss of loved ones. Trouble and death were to her ambrosia, and she never sang so loud and true as she did at a funeral.

Mama didn't care for her. They'd had a falling-out years before, when we lived in town. It had to do with Mama's not being small-town and Mrs. Rice's deciding she was stuck-up. Mama had lived in Montgomery, and it was there she'd been courted by Sheldon Maynard, the boy from Pluma who'd left his home town to go be in the Great War. I've heard Mama tell he was so good-looking in his soldier suit she didn't even think, just said yes to whatever he asked her.

The Andersons had been a middling family in Montgomery, neither high nor low. All that was left of them then was Mama and her brother Earl. Now there was Uncle Earl and Aunt Olive and their two children, Lucien and Alice. The war over—and, typically, Papa didn't even get to France, which I lied about when we read *In Flanders Fields* in school—he and Mama settled down in Pluma, where Papa worked at the dry goods store owned by Mr. Wadsworth. Nothing much happened to them, I gather, except life, but they didn't manage that very well. Mama didn't like small-town ways, with everybody knowing to the minute when she put her clothes on the line and to the penny how much Papa made. Maybe out of fret and boredom she gave herself airs. However that was, she made few friends. Papa left Mr. Wadsworth's store and tried farming on a place he'd bought with Mama's little bit of family money. (Uncle Earl had taken the family house; he was in the insurance business in Montgomery.) Papa didn't know farming, expected things to do themselves, which they don't, least of all on a farm. So the farm was soon lost and we wound up on that piece of sorry land belonging to Mr. Petrie. Negroes had lived in the house before us, and Mama scoured everything before we moved in.

I don't blame Mama and Papa, but in the long run it's better to be ugly and strong than pretty and weak, as they were. You expect less. One of the worst things about failure is that it gives people like Mrs. Rice so much satisfaction. When she first heard Mama was sick, she came out with her Bible pictures and both daughters, and they sat around with their hands in their laps and their eyes going everywhere to count the poorness of the way we lived. Mama discouraged their coming again.

Mrs. Rice had tried to stir up a fuss when Jim didn't start school at six, first coming to see Mama, who told her pretty quick to mind her business, and then calling me out of class one day to ask me a lot of personal questions. But I took on Mama's manners, short of being impudent, and gave her nothing to satisfy. The next she had to do with us was Mama's funeral, where she was in her best singing voice. She also clucked over Jim and me and said she would keep her eye on us.

She did.

We had few visitors, but she came now and then; and because she considered me still a child, went through the house inspecting everything and lifting pot lids on the stove as if it was her perfect right. But I'd long ago learned to keep house. Our beds were neatly made, and I kept a clean kitchen.

Mrs. Rice knew how Papa was about things, and I could see she was just waiting her chance to take us in hand. Like many, she thought the young had no feelings that mattered, and she said to people in town but so I could hear:

"Poor Mrs. Maynard dying of cancer through that sorry man's neglect! Her children would be better off in the Orphans' Home." That's why I hated her; that's why I was afraid of her.

It was also from that I got to calling Jim "Orphan Jim" when he was sassy or when he kept too much inside himself like I wasn't there. It was the only thing I could say that would rouse him.

"I'm not an orphan!" he'd holler.

"Are so!" I'd holler back, spiteful as I could be.

"If I'm an orphan, so are you!"

"Nosiree! I'm a grown girl who can take care of herself, but you're nothing but a little shirttail orphan! Orphan Jim! Orphan Jim!"

It always wound up with his trying to kick or hit or bite me and with me having to hold him till he got quiet. I wouldn't turn him loose till he promised not to fight me. Even so, he didn't always keep his promise.

Because of Mrs. Rice, and because of what Mr. Petrie had said about our getting off his place, I decided now was the time for me to hit the grit and head out from what I'd never thought of as home.

Where?

I could go anywhere I pleased, since there would be only me, and thinking that made me feel big as a tree and free as a frog. I'd just begin walking one day and follow where the wind blew. I'd sleep in the woods or somebody's barn. When I got hungry I could sweep somebody's house or wash their dishes for a meal. I'd work for my food and keep my self-respect and freedom to go when and wherever.

Papa had no kinfolk. He was an "orphan" too. My only other kin was Uncle Earl Anderson and his family in Montgomery. They'd all come to Mama's funeral, but

Uncle Earl had come by himself when he had the stone put on Mama's grave. (He did it because he knew Papa would keep putting it off and couldn't afford it anyway.)

I considered going to Montgomery because I had never been there. Mama had talked about it, and I was curious to see where she'd been a girl. But it scared me because of Uncle Earl. When he'd come with the gravestone, he had a little talk with me alone. Papa threw up his hands and said yes-go-ahead but not to expect him to stand around and watch a stone put on top of poor Mama. So off he went. I made Jim go with us though, and when it was in place, he squatted by the grave a long time and traced the letters of Mama's name and the dates of her life with his fingers. It was then Uncle Earl said if we were ever in real bad shape to remember he was Mama's brother and let him know.

Even as he said it, he looked guilty, and I knew why. I wouldn't call Uncle Earl the most outgoing and generous man on earth, but compared to Aunt Olive he was Santa Claus and Jesus rolled into one. Aunt Olive was a sour, grudging, grumbling woman. She had two topics of conversation: what everything cost and her children. Lucien was a year younger than me, and Alice was a year older than Jim. They hated us, and we hated them the few times they stopped by Pluma in their touring car to spend an hour or two with Mama. Lucien was a sneak, and Alice acted like the sole purpose of her existence was to keep her dress clean.

Maybe I'd hitchhike out to California and be a movie star. Movie stars didn't have to be pretty. Look at Marie Dressler and Polly Moran. I'd never seen a picture show. There wasn't one in Pluma or any place near. But we all knew about movie stars because some of the older girls brought movie magazines with them to school. Maybe I'd

9

head for New York, where all the rich people lived. It was enough for the moment to know I could go. Papa would have to take hold of himself with me gone and look after Jim. Anyway, that wasn't my concern; I wasn't Jim's mama. I would have to go before school started in September, and that was soon.

Then, lo and behold, Papa just up and left us.

I didn't worry when he stayed out the first night; he'd done that plenty of times since Mama died. But when he didn't come home in the morning, nor all that day, I got fidgety, and when the second and third nights came and went without him, I walked into town by myself without telling Jim why. I went straight to the depot and asked the men who loafed around the steps when they'd last seen Papa. He always headed for them, I knew, when he went in, knowing they were no better than he was. They didn't tell me anything helpful. I went to the dry goods store and asked Mr. Wadsworth, but he hadn't seen Papa.

So I went back home, worrying. We had a little meal and a little flour and some salt pork and the chickens. A few peas and squash and tomatoes were still bearing in the garden. But that was all.

Of course the news got around. I couldn't very well ask about Papa without people saying we didn't know where he was. So I wasn't surprised next day when Mrs. Rice drove up in her car with the school principal, Miss Ada Hopper. They got out and because of Miss Ada I asked them politely to come in. Jim tried to slip away, but I told him to stay, and for once he minded.

"Where's your daddy?" Mrs. Rice asked, all innocence.

"He's not home," I told her.

"When was he home last?" she then asked, and when I

didn't answer, she gave a quick look to Miss Ada and added, "You mean you can't remember?"

"Yes, ma'am," I said. "A day or so ago."

"Don't you know where he is, Gertrude?" Miss Ada asked me.

I wouldn't hedge with Miss Ada. She was a severe old maid, but she'd always been fair to me at school. "No, ma'am."

Miss Ada frowned, but as if she was concerned, not being hateful. "You children can't stay out here by yourselves."

"Oh, we're all right," I assured her. "I take care of Jim. Don't I, Jim?" Jim stared at the two ladies, lips out, pouting. "I cook for us. We got plenty to eat. You must have noticed the chickens when you drove in, Mrs. Rice, for you nearly ran over that old Rhode Island Red rooster. Mr. Petrie comes by to see us. We're getting along just fine, you can see, and Papa will be back soon."

"If you don't know where he is, you sure can't know when or if he'll be back," Mrs. Rice said. "It's my belief you'll never see him again."

Miss Ada was looking at Jim. "When school opens," she said, "you'll be starting first grade."

Jim nodded his head, interested for the first time in what was being said.

"Well, at least and at last we can all agree about that!" Mrs. Rice said with a mean smile. She looked again at Miss Ada before she continued. "Everything has been arranged. This very morning we have been to see Mr. Petrie, and he assures us our worst fears are all too well founded. You live like gypsies, hand to mouth, mother dead and no father to act like a father. So there's only one thing to do and we're going to see to that. Miss Hopper and I are driving this very minute over to Wadlow to make arrangements for you both to live in the Home there. You'll be better off."

Jim ran out, and I didn't have the heart to try to stop him. I told them about Uncle Earl in Montgomery and what he'd said about letting him know when we got real hard up, but Mrs. Rice said, "Fiddle. He's got a family of his own to support. I had a few words with his wife at the funeral. A thoroughly nice woman, but she said with your mama dead, they'd never be coming this way again."

I argued, I pled. I got so mad I nearly cried. But Miss Ada was firm, and Mrs. Rice was victorious. A lot was said on both sides, but a big argument like we had is mostly people saying the same things over and over. Whatever I said, Mrs. Rice said, "No, it's settled." When they left, I went to look for Jim. He was standing under the peach tree in the back yard, waiting. I took him by the shoulders and shook him good and hard. "Why'd you run out like that?" I asked, and shook him again harder, trying to make him cry for both of us; but he just stood there and took it, looking down at the ground until I let him go and went back into the house.

Nowadays it may be different, but back then the idea of going into any orphans' home was about the worst thing a child could think of. It was a bad dream of cruel adults and hungry children who were punished whether they were good or not; of cold, crowded rooms and no place or time to be by yourself. I don't know where we got such notions, but all children had them. The very words "Orphans' Home" could make the worst child shiver and feel grateful toward his parents.

Well, I for one wasn't going into any orphans' home. I decided to leave that very night. Miss Ada and Mrs. Rice would be back, maybe not tomorrow but before the end of the week, and then it would be too late.

I put Jim out of my mind, telling myself again I wasn't his mama and he'd be better off in a Home than following me where the wind blew. At least he'd have a bed to sleep in at night, and clothes to wear, and food of some kind to put into his stomach regularly; and they'd send him to school. He'd like school; he was a quick-minded boy, much as he aggravated me most of the time. I had liked school well enough myself.

I tried to act natural the rest of the day, only when I cooked supper I fried extra fatback and made biscuits. I'd carry the cold meat and biscuits with me when I went; they'd keep me from starving a day or so, I reckoned. I had decided not to go near people right at first for fear somebody would know me and try to turn me around toward home.

I thought Jim would never go to bed. It was like he knew what I planned. But finally off he went, and as soon as I heard him sleeping I put on my best dress and shoes and wrapped my biscuits and meat in a clean dishcloth, blew out the lamp, and slipped out of the house. It was a dark night, but that suited me. I'd walk a few miles away from Pluma before finding a place to sleep. I might even walk all night, just to get clean away, and sleep when I felt like it next day.

The dogs barked when I went past Mr. Petrie's house, but I kept right on and they quieted down. Country dogs bark at a lot of things and nobody pays attention unless they keep it up.

I had got well past Mr. Tom Hartley's farm, which was two miles from us, when I stopped in the middle of that dirt road and started cussing. I didn't know many words, but I did the best I could with what I knew. I don't think I'd ever been so mad in my life, not even that morning with Mrs. Rice.

It was Jim I was mad with. Oh, I didn't care about him. His being my brother cut no ice. He was nothing but a nuisance, a mama's baby that had lost its mama. But when I pictured him waking up in that house tomorrow morning, I knew I had to go back. I said he was quick-minded, and he was, but not in commonsense ways. Any average boy would have the gumption, left by himself, to go to Mr. Petrie. But I could just see Jim sitting there all day wondering what had become of me and waiting for somebody to come find him and tell him what to do. Thinking about it, I didn't just find him a nuisance and an aggravation. I hated him the way you can only hate close kin.

I turned around and walked back, half hoping I'd find him awake, needing to pee or something. I'd have felt better if he'd been out in the yard squawling his head off, scared of the dark. But no-sir, he was in his bed sound asleep.

CHAPTER 3

Jim lay stiff as a board on his bed, eyes shut, but I knew he was awake.

"Open your eyes, Jim. —Jim, it's Christmas morning! There's a tree and a hundred presents under it. —Jim! Look out the window, it's snowing!"

He flopped over on his stomach and scrunched up into himself, tight as a doodlebug when you touch it with a straw.

"Get up, Orphan Jim! They've come to haul you off to the Orphans' Home!" I shook his feet. He kicked me hard as he could, rolling onto his back, his eyes blazing open.

"Get away from me, Hateful!"

"What's got into you?"

"You left me last night!"

"What?"

"I woke up and you was gone!"

"I might have stepped out to the privy—"

"You don't put on your Sunday dress to go the privy!"

"There it is *there*, Smarty!" I pointed to the nail on the wall where it hung.

"It wasn't last night."

"I'm not going to stand here and listen to sass," I told him. "Dumb little boy! I've been making plans for us, but if you don't want to hear them—! If you'd *prefer* going to the Orphans' Home and letting them beat you and make you sleep with ten other dirty little boys, with not one mildewed maggoty biscuit to share among you—well, all right, you can just go ahead!" I stomped out.

When I stepped into the back yard, the chickens came clucking around me. They remembered when they got fed early every morning and evening. I hadn't fed them regular for a long time, just when I figured we could spare the corn meal. We had no proper chicken feed so I mixed meal with a little water to make a thick dough for them.

Jim didn't lose much time getting into his overalls. He came running from the house, but when he got to me, stopped sudden, not having thought ahead what he'd say. Finally he just said, "What?"

"What?" I mocked him, turning my head sideways and rolling my eyes like I was simple.

"What did you say about the Orphans' Home?"

I let him wait a minute, like I was studying on something. I then said, "You see these chickens? What you think I'm going to do with them?"

"Feed them?"

I snorted. "Kill them! They're going to feed us." I crossed the yard and went through the kitchen door. "You hungry?" I said, knowing he was right behind me.

He said he was. Opening the cloth that still held my going-away meat and biscuits, I made two sandwiches and handed him one. We began to eat, standing up. Jim wasn't a big eater, and cold fatback and biscuits didn't often tempt him, but I had his attention, and maybe hope gave him appetite.

"You want to go live in that Orphans' Home?" I asked.

"No!" Biscuit crumbs flew out of his mouth.

"Don't make a mess," I said, and he swept up the crumbs with his fingers. "*I'm* not going to any Home, I can tell you. I'm grown and that's only for younguns. Maybe you'd be better off there."

"No, I wouldn't. What you going to do?"

"I'm not certain I should tell you."

"Tell me, Trudy!"

Keeping a solemn face I said, "I'm going to say kiss-my-tail to Mrs. Rice."

That shocked him so, he went to giggling, but when he got his breath again said, "Spit on her warts!"

I hit him to remind him he was a child. "I'm going to leave this farm and this town."

"You don't believe Papa will come home?"

I shook my head. "You want to stay and wait for him?"

"No. Where we going?"

"I haven't said *you're* going anywhere. But if I do, we'll head for Montgomery, where Uncle Earl lives."

"I'm scared of Aunt Olive. I hate Alice and Lucien."

I said, "They're our kinfolks, and Uncle Earl said he'd take care of us if we needed him to."

"When did he tell you such a thing?" Jim asked suspiciously.

"That day he brought the tombstone for Mama."

His lips went out in a pout.

"If you don't like my planning, you can stay here," I said.

"I'll go," he said quick.

"I haven't said you can."

"If you go, you got to take me with you!"

"I don't have to do anything," I said. "I'm grown now and free to go and come as I please. You're an orphan that has to do as he's told."

"I won't!"

"Then you shan't go with me."

I let him pout another little while and think it over, waiting until he said with argument in his voice, "Trudy, you can't—"

"Don't tell me what Trudy can and can't do. You may as well know right now you're a burden. I did start off by myself last night, because I wanted to be free of you. But if you go with me, you have to do what I tell you. No sassing. You'll have to help out too, not just wait for victuals to be handed to you. You'll have to do dirty things if I tell you, and not make trouble about it. You understand?"

He grunted.

"That's not enough to say. You got to promise to mind me." I gave him a minute to think, watching his eyes go blank and stubborn. "If you don't promise, you can't go, and if you don't keep your promise, you can't stay with me. You can wait for Mrs. Rice to come get you here, or just sit around till you rot."

After another minute of hard thinking he said, "I promise I'll help out."

"And do what I tell you," I insisted.

"And mind," he said like he was giving up his last hope.

"Now, you remember that, because we may get into some tight places where I'll have to think for both of us. If that happens, I can't have you asking why or dragging your butt. Before now, every time I've had to kill a chicken for us to eat, you've run off and hid. You won't do that today. We're going to kill these chickens together, and I'm going to fry them and make some flour hoecakes. We'll take them with us, and not much else." I had a kettle of water on the stove with the fire made up. I mixed some meal and water in a pan and went to the door. "Come on," I said.

I had decided to kill just the younger chickens; there were four of them. The others were too old and tough to fry, and I couldn't wait around for them to bake in the oven.

In the yard I told Jim what I wanted him to do, and he nodded his head to show he understood. He was white in the face, but I could see he was determined to keep his promise, at least to start with.

I dropped a wad of dough, and the chickens came running. It was easy to catch two of them and hand one to Jim. It cackled and flapped its wings trying to get away. "Hold it away from your face!" I warned him, for it was trying to peck him. "Get hold of his legs and turn him upside down and if he fights, hold on tight." He was clumsy about it, but he did it. I set my pan out of reach of the other chickens and wrung the neck of the one I still held. When I could feel that it was broken, I dropped him, took the one Jim was holding, and wrung its neck too. He stared at the two of them flopping around on the ground and looked like he wanted to run off.

"Now we're going to do it again," I said.

"I bet they won't come back."

"A chicken's got no feelings." I dropped more dough from the pan, and here they came, ignoring the two still jerking around, busy dying.

We grabbed two more, Jim helping this time, and I wrung their necks. Then I fed the rest of the dough to the others, which seemed to make Jim feel better. I explained step by step what we had to do next. As soon as the water boiled, we'd dip the chickens to loosen their feathers so we could pick them. I told him we had to wait until we were sure they were dead—he shivered when I said that—because if we didn't, they'd look red instead of white when we picked them. And the water had to be really boiling, and we had to hold the chicken in the water just so long and no longer, otherwise the feathers wouldn't come off, or else feathers and skin would come off together.

He did his best, but it wasn't much good. I had to go over the one he plucked to the three of mine; but I could see he was trying, and maybe he'd improve. Whatever else, it was a lesson in minding me. I made him stay with me while I cut up the chickens and threw their guts and feet and heads into the yard. I thought he was going to be sick when the other chickens ran and fought over the mess, but I told him that's the way chickens were; they'd eat anything including each other.

When I was frying the pieces, he began to look a little better. Even so, he shook his head, watching me turn the pieces in the skillet, and said he wasn't going to eat any.

"Yes, you will," I told him, "when you get hungry."

When the chicken cooled I put it and the flour hoecakes in two clean buckets we had used sometimes for syrup and sometimes for berry picking. Then I took a hand basket and packed a few clothes for us. We didn't have much, but

I didn't intend to take all we had, just clean drawers, shirts, and a pair of short pants for him, a dress or two for me.

Jim was my shadow every minute, maybe thinking I'd slip off without him. Maybe he was actually trying to help. I wanted to tell him to get out of the way, to sit down and count his fingers till I had everything ready, but I bit my tongue and kept quiet, knowing it was good practice for him to attend to what I was doing. I didn't pause or hesitate one second. I was afraid that if I did, somebody would stop me, and I had to get away from Pluma and the farm and all that went before that morning. The only thing I couldn't get rid of was Jim, but I was resigned to that for the time being. What Jim didn't know was in my mind was I'd deliver him to Uncle Earl and leave him, going on by myself.

I thought of taking a pan to cook in, but gave it up. We had to go light, so the only thing I took from the kitchen was a cup.

The last thing: I put on shoes and made Jim put on his, telling him he had to wear or carry them, and they were easier to wear, though he complained.

All was done: the two buckets of victuals ready and the basket of clothes tucked in with a towel. Our clock had stopped in the excitement, but I could tell by the shadows it wasn't yet noon. I think I'd have died if I'd heard the sound of a car coming, anybody's car at all. I went to the barn and turned the mule loose. I didn't care a thing about him; we'd never given him a name. He could fend for himself and find his way to Mr. Petrie's.

I knew a back way from our place across Mr. Petrie's fields and through some woods to the graveyard where Mama was buried. There was no risk in our going there because it was the direction away from town. The church had burned down long ago, but there was still plenty of room left for graves. It was in open country with no farmhouse near. I took the basket in one hand and a bucket in the other, giving Jim the second bucket to carry, and we struck out without looking back. Jim wasn't surprised when we came in sight of the graveyard an hour after leaving, though I hadn't said we'd stop there. We set our things down under a tree and found Mama. Jim squatted by the grave and fingered the carving again, letters and numbers she'd taught him. When I told him it was time to go, he patted the slab before picking up the bucket and following me.

We cut into the woods again, and I waited till Jim complained twice of being tired before I slackened my pace. I didn't let us stop to rest for another quarter hour. Then we ate what was left of the cold biscuits and greasy meat I'd cooked the night before. I made us go on before he was ready. I had to be hard with him, I decided, particularly at first. He whimpered but didn't resist for fear I'd leave him, as I'd told him I would if he made any fuss or trouble.

I kept us to the shade as long as I could, because it was hot walking, and so nobody could see us to tell who we were, but late in the afternoon we had to join the main road north if we ever expected to get anywhere. Luckily, we were offered a ride by an old Negro man who was taking his wagon empty from the cotton gin back to his farm. I told him we were on our way to our grandmother's, figuring he hadn't read "Little Red Riding Hood." I was to discover later that saying that satisfied people and shut them up. The old man was sleepy anyhow and didn't ask any questions. He took us four miles before he had to turn off to his place. By then I felt we'd done pretty good for our first day.

We'd put a fair distance between us and Pluma, and I vowed to Jim and myself nobody was going to catch up with us now.

Those early days I kept thinking somebody was after us, following and ready to throw a cage over us and take us Away, take us Back. It dawned on me gradually that nobody was following us because nobody cared.

CHAPTER 4

The first night out wasn't bad. For one thing, it *was* the
first. There was the pride I felt at having done something
about us instead of waiting to be told to come here, go
there, say thank you. I picked a dry place off the road under
some pine trees, the kind of place if you were passing in a
car somebody was bound to say, "Wouldn't that be a nice
place for a picnic?" The day had been fair and hot. That
late in summer the ground didn't lose its heat during the
night, so we weren't cold. And we were tired enough to
sleep standing up, like birds on a branch.

We washed our faces and hands and feet in the same

creek we drank water from, dipping the cup I'd brought. I didn't know where it came from or where it was going, but the water was running free and in the cup looked almost clear. The cold chicken and our hoecake tasted good. I couldn't help smiling when I saw Jim smacking away, almost eating his fingers with the drumstick they held, he was so hungry.

"To think," I said, "a live chicken was running around this morning on that thing you got in your hand now." He didn't stop eating or slacken his greed, but his eyes cussed me over his greasy mouth. When he'd got all the meat and gristle off the bone, he threw it away and stuffed his mouth full of hoecake. Still chewing, he broke wind.

"Did you step on a frog?" I asked politely.

"I pooted," he said.

"In future," I said, "please don't do such a thing as that while I'm eating my supper, because if you do, I'll beat you to death."

Like he was telling me a big secret he said, "I hate you, Miss Biggety," and lay down and went to sleep before I was through eating. I pressed the lid back tight on the food bucket we'd eaten from. Last thing I heard was mosquitoes, but I knew it was hopeless trying to slap at them out in the open like we were. We'd eaten. Now it was their turn.

The next two days we walked and ate chicken and hoecake. Nobody gave us a ride, and I didn't press because we hadn't come all that way from Pluma and there was still a risk somebody would see us who knew who we were, or would ask too many questions and find out. We didn't stop at any farmhouses either, for the same reason. We went through two towns, but they were little and nobody paid us any mind because we didn't stop, just kept on going. The end of the second day we finished the victuals we'd brought with us, piecing them out with some apples I'd picked from a tree in a fallow field we passed. I threw one of the buckets away, but washed the other to take along, figuring there might be a use for it.

The third morning I was determined to get us a ride, so when we came to a filling station I walked us on a little piece beyond it and stopped in the shade where the man pumping gas wouldn't notice us. That way we'd have a chance of a ride with whoever came in to buy gas, I reckoned, because they wouldn't be going too fast to stop when they left.

Things were slow. For the longest time only one car stopped for gas, but didn't stop for us. Then a beat-up truck drew in by the pump, and I saw the driver get out and open the lid of the cold-drinks box and take the cap off an Orange Crush while the station man filled his tank. They didn't talk, and the driver was done with his drink and ready to pay by the time the man finished and wiped his hands on his overalls.

I took the basket and Jim the bucket and we stepped out of the shade where the driver could see us. Sure enough, he stopped the truck without cutting off his motor and leaned out to call, "You younguns want a ride?"

"Sure do," I told him.

"Well, come on." He opened the door, and we piled in. I put Jim next to him with me on the other side holding the basket in my lap; and off we went.

I told Jim to keep his feet out of the man's way, and I looked out the open window, enjoying the speed we were making. I don't suppose it was fast at all, but after walking as long as we had, anything with wheels would seem speedy. Jim was looking at the driver, admiring the way he drove, one hand kind of loose on the steering wheel, the other arm resting on the door ledge.

A mile on, the man said, "My name's Bud. What's y'all's?"

"I'm Gertrude. Trudy. This is my brother Jim."

Jim hit me on the arm. "I can say my own name." Turning to the man he said, "I'm Jim."

The man nodded matter-of-fact, like he understood Jim's not wanting a girl to speak for him, then said easy enough, although it was like a clap of thunder to my ears, "You chillun running away from home?"

"No, sir!" I rushed to say. "We're not. We're going to visit our grandma."

He nodded. "She know you're coming?"

"Why yes," I said. "She begged us to come see her some time, and we wrote her a letter saying we would."

"Where'd you mail your letter?" I was too smart for that and just sat still not answering. When I let my eyes slant toward the man, his lips were working a little like he was talking to himself. Then he hummed, and when he got done with the tune, said, "Don't get in a huff, sis. I run away from home myself when I wasn't much older than you."

"You did?" Jim said. That made things all right with him.

The man nodded and squeezed Jim's knee. "I was a damn sight older than you though, buddy."

"Well, we're not running away from home exactly," I said. "Where are you headed, mister?"

"Bud's enough. You'll find plenty of other people to 'mister.'"

"Well then, where you going, Bud?"

"Hauling this load of cotton seed to Mobile. I'll pick up

another load of something there and go on someplace else."

"You mean you're free to go any place you feel like?"

"It's my truck. I don't have to take a load if I don't like the destination."

Jim beamed at the man, and the man smiled at him like they were buddies.

"My ma died when I was eight," Bud said, "and my old man wasn't worth killing. He'd get drunk and lay out all night, then come home and whip all us younguns for no reason. I was the oldest and when I just couldn't put up with it no more I struck out. Never looked back, never been sorry."

"People treat you good?" I asked.

He shrugged. "Some good, some not. How 'bout you-all?"

I looked him over the best I could with the three of us sitting alongside each other. I wasn't so good at judging age, but he mustn't have been much over twenty. He was wearing khaki pants and a white shirt frayed and a little dirty at the collar, with his sleeves rolled up. He had a lot of black hair he'd tried to slick down but it fell every whichaway. He didn't look so bad. So I told him. I told him about Mama and the farm and Papa and Mr. Petrie. He frowned when I came to the part about Mrs. Rice and Miss Ada. When I told him about Uncle Earl, his face got in a study for a while and he drove along not saying anything. Then abruptly he said, "Does this Uncle Earl of yours know you're coming? And don't tell me you wrote him a letter if you didn't." I said he didn't know but he'd offered to take care of us that last time he came by himself to Pluma. "His wife, your Aunt Olive, she don't have any idea what you got in mind though, does she?" That sunk

us in gloom some little time. Then Bud commenced singing an old song even we knew called "Little Brown Jug."
Jim and I both joined in here and there, and we all laughed
and were friends. Jim spelled out some of the road signs
and billboards we passed, things like Clabber Girl Baking
Powder and Bull Durham tobacco. We rode on that way
feeling pretty good until Bud said, "I'm getting hungry.
What about you younguns? I'll set you up."

I nudged Jim to be quiet and I didn't say anything either.

Bud said, "You don't have to go all proud with me, sis."

"We had fried chicken last night," I said.

"Yes, and the night before too," Jim said. "We been eating nothing but fried chicken. I can't abide fried chicken!"

Bud whooped, and I had to tell him what we'd done
about the chickens, and then he whooped some more.
"Why didn't you cut up the mule and fry him too?" he
asked, and that got me and Jim to laughing with him.
"Well, I won't offer you fried chicken, but there's a cafe up
the road run by a lady named Miss Rosalie and she makes
mighty good hamburgers. You ever had a hamburger,
Jim?"

"No, sir," Jim said.

"I have," I said. Jim looked at me but didn't dispute my
word.

"Well, Jim," Bud said, "I'll be proud to introduce you to
one of the best things there is in life."

When we got there, the cafe turned out to be a neat
white-painted house with some tourist cabins back of it.
We left our things in the truck and followed Bud. He went
in banging the screen door like he owned the place, calling
out, "It's me again, Miss Rosalie!" to the lady leaning over
the counter smoking a cigarette and reading a *True Story*

magazine, with a little white radio playing music on a shelf back of her. I had pictured Miss Rosalie different from the way she looked. She wasn't young exactly, but her yellow dress fit her tight. She had yellow hair that I knew was from peroxide even though I'd never seen anybody before with a dyed head of hair. Her face and arms were fat and red. She had a gold tooth she liked to show when she laughed, and she laughed a whole lot with Bud. Everything he said seemed to tickle her. She had, I reckon, the biggest titties I ever saw on a woman in my life. When she laughed, they shook like an earthquake, and that just seemed to encourage Bud to cut the fool and make her laugh more.

But finally they quieted down some and Bud introduced us to her as his cousins. She winked at him but didn't deny it, just saying, "Hey there," real friendly to both of us and asking if we wanted to sit at a table to eat or would the counter suit. I said the table, but Jim said the counter. We sat at the counter because Bud said it was easier for him to talk to Miss Rosalie while she fried the hamburgers. She put six on the griddle at Bud's order, and they were big ones too. Jim was studying a cherry pie under a dome you could see through when Bud saw him and said, "You can have some of that too when you had enough hamburgers. Which you like best, cherry or raisin?"

That whole affair was one of the best times I'd had in my life. Bud ate four hamburgers; Jim ate two and had two pieces of pie, one of the cherry and one of the raisin to show no partiality. I had three hamburgers and a Baby Ruth instead of pie. Bud drank Coca-Colas and Jim had two Nehi chocolate drinks and I had two glasses of milk, which I'd missed ever since we sold the cow. Everybody laughed and were friends. Miss Rosalie shared the good time with us until some other truck drivers came in, and a couple wanting to rent a tourist cabin, and she was too busy to fool with us.

When we were through eating and had been sitting there just talking for a while, I noticed Bud was looking out the front window at his truck more and more often. When Miss Rosalie had a few slack minutes he motioned her to the back of the cafe and they had a little talk. At first she shook her head and frowned, but then she agreed to what he said, although reluctant. They sauntered back and he paid her for all we'd had to eat. Motioning us with his head, he led us on out. When we got to the truck, Jim grabbed the door and opened it, climbing up on the seat like he lived there. Bud looked kind of embarrassed, though he smiled as he reached in and hauled Jim down to the ground again. "This is where we split up, younguns," he said. "I turn south half a mile down the road, and you-all are headed north; ain't that right?"

"That's right," I said.

"I've explained the thing to Miss Rosalie, and she's promised to look out for a good ride for you. So when I leave, you go back in with your things and just wait there till she fixes you up. All right now?"

"Yes, sir," I said.

"Well." He shifted his weight from one leg to the other and clapped his hands together. "You chillun take care of yourself and stay out of mischief." He winked big and swung himself up into the truck, handing down our basket and bucket. Jim was frowning and pouting, so Bud reached and hit him friendly on the head before slamming the truck door. He started the motor, then lifted his hand from the steering wheel to wave and said, "See y'all!"

Off he went, us watching him till the road turned. I picked up our basket and handed Jim the empty bucket.

"I want to go with Bud," Jim said.

"Well, you can't!" I said, sounding mean even to myself.

Miss Rosalie wasn't so friendly when we went back in. Oh, she kept her promise to Bud, but she gave us none of her time, and she appeared to have done her laughing for the day. She told us to sit at a little table at the back where we wouldn't be in the way, until she found us a ride. After a while Jim had to go to the toilet and when he came back and sat down again, he took the ketchup bottle from the table and began to drip ketchup into his palm and lick it. The cafe was empty by that time except for us. Miss Rosalie had the radio turned up loud, and she looked over from some kind of figuring she was doing at the cash register and caught Jim at it. Flying over, she grabbed the bottle away from him and put the cap back on, then slapped his hands and told us to touch nothing else or she'd make us leave. I wasn't surprised when a little later she got us a ride with a man that stopped in for a Coca-Cola and some salted peanuts he dropped in the bottle as he drank. He didn't carry us far, just far enough for her to be rid of us. He didn't talk to us, but to be polite I asked him how much he weighed, and he said a hundred and eighty-three.

CHAPTER 5

I wouldn't have missed meeting Bud for anything, but after riding with him that day, though we'd gone east, we'd also veered south, and he'd taken us farther south than we were when we left Pluma. Also, his being good to us the way he had, made us more dissatisfied with each other than ever. By next morning we pure-and-T despised each other. We woke up aching from the hard ground we'd slept on, and had nothing to eat. There were few cars passing and none of them even slowed as they went by.

We walked for nearly two hours before we came to a house sitting just off the road. There were woods and fields all around it, but it didn't look like a farm. It almost didn't look like a house, because the front porch was entirely covered, front and sides, with heavy vines.

After we'd stepped off the road, I stopped. Jim stopped too, not looking at me or the house, just waiting. I was undecided whether to go to the front door or the back. I'd be begging for the first time. I walked a little closer and stopped again, Jim doing the same, like my shadow. There wasn't a sign of life, no smoke, no noise of chickens or dog. Maybe nobody was home or nobody lived there but lizards and mice, though the place didn't have an empty look so much as lonely.

My next walking brought us up to the porch. I was just standing there with Jim behind me, wondering what to do next and more than half inclined to tuck tail and go on along the road when somebody pulled the vines apart not two feet from my face and said, "You've come! You've come at last!"

I jumped, and Jim jumped with me, but the voice, a woman's, said, "Don't run away when I've waited so long!"

She sounded so plaintive I inched back to look at her. She appeared old to me, though she may have been no more than forty. It was a plain, tallowy face with eyes looking out of hollows. Her black hair was parted in the middle and tied in a knot at the back. A hair net was stretched over all from front to back. She said the one thing most calculated to hold me. "Are you hungry?"

"Yes, ma'am," I said, and my shadow echoed, "Yes, ma'am."

"I was hoping you would be when you got here." She stood up, left her chair rocking, and came to the steps. Unlatching the screen door, then latching it again, she looked at us good and hard. "Better not come through the house. Go around to the back porch and wash your face and hands first so I can see you."

We hadn't done much about washing ourselves since we left the farm, and I realized then it must show. I was ashamed I hadn't been stricter with both of us and by the time she met us at the back porch I was ready to say, "We must look a sight. Haven't had time, traveling; haven't thought to—"

"Put your basket and bucket down on the steps. While you're still in the yard dust your clothes like this." She gave a brisk demonstration on her clean dress, and we copied her, making a great flapping to-do. There was a rickety washstand on the porch. She went to it and poured water from a bucket into an old-timey bowl. Indicating towel and washrag on a wall nail and soap in a saucer she said to me, "If you're going to be my children, you'll have to be clean children. I won't have you hiding behind dirt. No telling who you might be. Come into the kitchen when you're ready for inspection."

She went in, and I heard her banging pans and clinking dishes as I wet the rag in the bowl and soaped it good and started to work on me and Jim. I scoured our faces, hands, and arms until I nearly took the skin off. Then I combed the rattails out of our hair with Mama's old tortoise comb I'd brought in the basket of clothes. It was the only thing of hers I had now. When I judged us fit, I knocked hard at the door and pushed Jim in front of me into the kitchen. She turned from the stove, where she was frying eggs, and stared at us, her eyes going cautious. "Well, sit down," she said, indicating tall straight chairs at the big table in the middle of the room. She went over to a cupboard at the side and brought out a great big black book, slamming it down on the table.

35

"What's your name? I've forgot."

"Gertrude and Jim," I said, and noticed Jim didn't seem to mind my answering for him that time.

"When you're asked your name," she said, "always give your last name. The first doesn't signify."

"Maynard," I said. "Gertrude and James Maynard."

"That doesn't sound right to me," she said, cocking her head doubtfully. "Are you sure?" Without waiting for an answer, which was just as well because I didn't have one ready for her, she said, all innocence now, "Look at my scrapbook and tell me what you think of it."

Jim scraped his chair over to mine as I opened the book. It was full of pictures and stories cut out from a newspaper.

"That's Lindy," Jim said, recognizing the man in the first picture. Charles Lindbergh was still every boy's hero for what he had once done; even country children like Jim knew his face.

She gave a funny laugh, as if it was for herself alone. "You'd have to admit that much." She left the stove and came to stand behind our chairs and look over our heads at the book. "Poor man.—Why do I say that? He should have been more careful of the baby. Poor angel! I never one minute trusted Betty Gow. People like that don't merit the responsibility of a beautiful child. She was an ignorant immigrant—but you know that; of course you do. Although you might claim everybody knows it because it's been in the newspapers. My cousin Ruth in Opelika sends me all the stories from the newspapers she can lay hands on, knowing I see nothing like that here. If that baby had been mine—right over their very heads it happened. Oh, if that baby had been mine, I tell you, I'd not have left it alone one minute of the night or day."

I had broken out in sweat. Though he couldn't really

36

read, Jim was turning pages in the book as if he was afraid to look around at either one of us. Smoke billowed up from the stove, and the awful stink of burning eggs filled the kitchen.

"They said it was me, you know. Oh, yes, they came here, ten of them in two big cars and asked me every question you can think of and some I'd be ashamed to repeat to you; but I can prove to a certainty where I've been and what I've been doing every hour of every day of my entire life. Can you do that? Not many can boast that and speak true, but I can and do because I always knew they'd come after me and accuse me of it. They looked in the closets and under each bed and table. They drained the well. They set traps for me everywhere, but I was too smart for them. They wanted me to talk to Jafsie. *Jafsie!* Have you noticed what funny names they all have? Big as you please they said they were going to drive me north and face me with Jafsie, but I got the horsewhip I keep under my bed at night—"

I had edged my chair back and away some. "I think the eggs must be done," I said, knowing how foolish it was to say but at a loss to say anything sensible.

"Is that all you can think of with that poor baby's fate in the balance?" The sallow, tallowy face turned purple as she grabbed up the frying pan from the stove and emptied it on the floor. "There! You can eat slop, you unfeeling pigs!" There was a clatter and I guessed Jim had fallen off his chair, but I was watching her too close to check on him. Her voice went on, low and cunning. "You thought I didn't know who you were, didn't you? I knew the second I saw you creeping off the road trying to catch me by surprise—stealing up on me like a game of one-two-three-four-five-six-seven-eight-nine-ten redlight! Why do you think I made you wash yourselves? So the disguise would come off! You're in with that Betty Gow, all of you Scotties from Scotland. You're the cook and butler, Elsie and Oliver Whateley, and don't you dare deny it! Oh, you all thought you were so smart. You know my weakness, so you disguised yourselves as children and came to find out what I know. Well, I know plenty, but I won't tell you a thing. I'll go to my grave with my secrets!"

Jim started to cry and ran out the back door. Having watched him go with her mouth open and oozing, she wheeled on me, the frying pan held over her head as a weapon. "He got away, but don't you run, you she-devil!" She swung the smoking pan at me, but I scrambled back, bumping into the table. To keep me from falling, my hands clutched out and found the scrapbook. I took it up to counter her skillet if she tried to use it against me again.

"That's why you came!" she screamed. "To steal the evidence!" She dropped the skillet and came at me with her claws raised. I swung the book at her to ward her off. She grabbed it from me, and I let go. Dropping to her knees, she forgot me, cradling the book in her arms and crooning to it. Keeping my eyes on her, I stepped over to the stove, but there wasn't anything on it fit to eat except some boiled potatoes in a pie pan. I grabbed that and went out fast as I could, pausing only to take our clothes basket.

Jim had gone to the road and stood there bawling like a calf. When he saw me coming, he commenced to run, but I called him and in a minute he stopped and waited. "Come on," I said, going by him and not even turning around to see if he followed. I knew he did because I could hear him sniffing. As soon as we went around a bend and were out of sight of the house, I stopped and held out the pan of potatoes. "See what I got?"

"I don't want any old potatoes," he said.

"Yes, you do," I told him. Setting the basket down, I leaned back on the bank beside the road and started to eat.

"I bet they're poison," Jim said.

"Well, if you see me drop dead, you'll know you're right." I finished the first potato and started on another. In a minute he came over and leaned on the bank beside me, taking a potato from the pan and gobbling it down. When we'd finished them I set the pan on top of the bank. "Maybe she'll find it," I said. "Let's go."

Jim had never been much to talk to—for me, that is, although I'd heard him go like a streak of lightning with Mama sometimes. But I'd have had to talk then if it had only been to myself. "She must have brooded herself crazy," I said. "We were all upset about it at school, don't you remember? Everybody brought stories and had a big lot to say. There wasn't nothing talked for the longest time but the Lindberghs. We all felt so sorry for them. Don't you recollect my talking to you and Mama about it?"

"I wish I had me a hamburger," Jim said.

I said, "Now just imagine her taking you for Oliver Whateley. You look more like Jafsie to me."

"I left the bucket back there," he said. "If you think I'm going to get it, you're crazy with the heat."

"I don't talk to orphans," I said, and broke into a run, he following behind bawling his head off.

CHAPTER 6

"Sissie, you ain't anything special, get that through your head. There's younger than you-all wandering the roads looking for a home or a handout. I see fifteen, twenty ever week." The fat man wiped sweat from his face with the inside of his elbow and sat down on the empty Coca-Cola crate in front of his store. Jim and I had walked up a few minutes before, late afternoon of the day after we got messed up with the crazy Lindbergh lady. We'd had just two short rides and nothing to eat. There were no late berries along the roadside and no fruit in the fields we passed, so we were real hungry. If we hadn't been, I wouldn't have had the nerve to march up to that man at his store and ask him for something, anything he could spare, I said. There was nothing but the store at the crossroads, and a gas pump in front.

"It just ain't reasonable to expect me to feed ever Sunbonnet Sue and Overall Tom that takes a notion to stop and beg. You can see that surely. Nobody got a nickel, hear them tell it." He stood up with an effort, and the Coca-Cola crate teetered and fell. As he walked through the door of the store still talking, we followed him. "Now, if you show me you're willing to do a little work, I may get softhearted. You're lucky, you might say, hittin' me just at this junction. Nigger I had helpin' me took a notion to move on to Birmingham. He wasn't worth killing, but now I got nobody. The boy don't look much, and you don't strike me a lot better. But if you want to make a liar of me, start in on this case of peas and stack 'em nice and even on the shelf back here. When you get done, if you ain't made a total failure of it, we'll see about the next thing."

"Yes, sir." I took a few seconds to size up the job and placed Jim to hand me the cans one at the time. The man watched us work, and when we were done took us over to the lattice wall that divided the main store from the back room. Just inside the back room there were two big barrels with spigots: one to sell kerosene, the other syrup, a nickel a quart each, he explained. The top of the syrup barrel was a glue of filth and spillings mixed together.

"There's a water tap and bucket in the toilet," the man said. "See if you can make this thing shine."

"Yes, sir."

It took a lot longer than stacking the case of peas, but we got it done, and he said, "While you got the bucket out, sprinkle some water over the floor to settle the dust and give her a good sweeping. Nigger didn't get to it before he left me yesterday."

We set to. Jim sprinkled, I swept.

When we were about half done, I heard the man say—he was at the front of the store near the door—"I wondered where you'd got off to, Lady. Come on inside." I looked around to see a fat white-and-brindle bulldog waddle through the door, dripping slobber as she hassled to help herself stand the heat. It struck me the dog and the man looked a lot alike, the way people and their dogs often do. "Where you been to, Lady; ain't you gonna tell?" His voice was whiney and lovey. "Or maybe you think it ain't any of my business, huh?" She looked at him noncommittally, hassling louder. "How'd you like a nice cool something; you'd like that, wouldn't you, Lady?"

Lady didn't show any sign, but the fat man went to the box where he kept bottled drinks cold and took out a chunk of ice. He put it in a dirty bowl on the floor I reckoned was hers, and she went to work on it. I had to sweep around her, and she growled deep in her chest when I got close. That tickled the man. Leaning over, he scratched her back and said, "That's right, Lady, you eat anybody up don't do like you say."

When we finished the sweeping we went out front to find the man. He was balanced on the Coca-Cola crate, and Lady was by him, hassling, but not so fast as she had. The man didn't look at us, just frowned to show he knew we were there. For a while we shifted from one foot to the other. A funny expression came over the man's face, and I could tell he was enjoying our standing uncertain like beggars. Finally he looked sly and said, "Y'all hungry?"

I said, "Yes, sir."

With a groan like he was put-upon, he set hands on

knees and got to his feet. We followed as he shuffled into the store. He went slow as he could without actually stopping but finally made it to the end of the long counter that ran the length of one side. There was a big, greasy, copper-colored can on it. Taking the smallest cardboard tray he had, ones like they used to sell loose lard in, he speared three oil sausages out of the can with a long fork. Then he reached back of him to a shelf and found a half loaf of bread. Hesitating, he said, "I reckon you younguns can have all of that."

I took it and opened it. It had mold on it, and he saw it did and turned his back, going on up front and outside again. I pinched off what mold I could, and we set to eating. We shared the sausage fifty-fifty, but I let Jim lick the tray. We were so hungry I don't think we tasted anything. I was still eating bread, not being too careful about the mold, when I heard a new voice and turned around to see a Negro woman charging through the lattice doorway from the back room. I sure hadn't seen her when I'd gone to get water from the toilet, but it was dark back there and so was she. This woman was screaming at Jim, "Git your hands out of that sausage can, you son of a bitch!"

Sure enough, without my noticing, Jim had slipped the lid off the oil sausage and reached in.

The fat man, hearing the commotion, came hustling back with his fat dog barking her head off. The woman picked up a flyswatter from the counter and slapped Jim's hands. "Thieving devil! Tramp shit! Son of a bitching bastard!"

The man, laughing fit to kill, worked his way between Jim and the woman, and I pulled Jim away. "What you catch 'em doing, Cora?"

"Stealing sausage!" She tried to reach around him to get

at us with the flyswatter. "Can't lie down and get my rest without you letting people come in and walk all over you."

"I gave them something for doing a little work."

"Give an inch, they take a mile!"

"I'm too soft-hearted," the man said, shaking his head sadly as he turned to us. "She cooks for me, and one thing and another."

"Oughtn't to be good to stray cats," the woman called Cora said. "They show gratitude by pissing on the flour sack." Her words seemed to whet her rage, and she recommenced flailing with the flyswatter.

That set the dog to growling and barking again, more like she meant business than before. The fat man barked too with laughter as the woman and dog took after us. Jim was already through the front door, and I was following. Last I heard was the man calling, "Sic 'em, Lady! Sic 'em, Cora!"

Down the road a way we found a patch of cucumbers that had been left to go wild. They were too big to be fit to eat and still hot from the sun, but we ate a few.

That night we slept against some baled hay in a field. At first light I woke up, feeling Jim trying to get under me. His whole body was shaking and felt hot as a stove. I knew the chills and fever meant he had malaria. Lord God, I thought, hating him, hating the world.

CHAPTER 7

I took everything out of the basket and wrapped it around Jim, but he still shook. I then went and stood in the road, determined to stop the first car that came by. I did, and it was a doctor. When you have to have something, sometimes you get it.

Instead of saying, "Where are you from? What are you doing here? Who are your folks?" he just followed me into the field, looked at Jim, slung him over his shoulder, and took him back to his car, me following with the basket of clothes I'd quick picked up off the ground.

When I say prayers—it comes to me sudden at irregular

times—I try to say one for that man. He was a young fellow then, Dr. Joe Tatum, with red hair and freckles on everything that showed: face, neck, the back of his hands. He set Jim on the rear seat and tucked his jacket around him like he was putting a baby to bed. Then we got in front and he drove off to the town he said was named Thebes. Since he didn't ask me any questions, I was full of answers. While I babbled out our whole history, he nodded occasionally like he already knew it by heart. The fat man had said we weren't anything special; I guess we weren't.

I'm always finding out things about myself, and when I do I feel like a fool for not having seen them before. I named my first boy Joe, although there were no Joes in my or my husband's family; the name just seemed to come to me. When he was little we used to call him "Tater" for fun because he had a passion for baked sweet potatoes. He'd toddle into the kitchen when he smelled them baking, his hands cupped to receive, and say, "Tater." I never thought of the connection till this day.

As we rode into town, Dr. Joe interrupted me. "I'm going to take y'all to the Methodist preacher's house. Reverend Abb Skinner—"

"Surely Jim's not that bad off!" I cried.

"No!" He looked startled. "He lives with his sister, Miss Verity. She keeps house for him. She's a *good* woman. She—"

"Oh, Lord!" I said, remembering Mrs. Rice in Pluma.

"You've got no call to be scared of her," he said. "I'm not much religious myself, but Miss Verity doesn't talk it, she does things to help people."

I bit my tongue and kept my counsel since he'd been good enough to pick us up.

"Your brother needs a bed and regular food and quinine.

I'll provide the quinine. You and Miss Verity can cook and nurse. You don't have it too, do you?"

"No, sir. Jim just got it. This is his first time. I had it last summer."

When we got there, he told me to stay in the car and watch Jim while he went to explain. It was then we both realized how early it was. Dr. Joe had been out all night with a patient dying of diphtheria, and of course I didn't know the time. Though I found out later Miss Verity was an early riser, she wasn't up yet. He'd knocked on the door a while before she opened it in a kimono and her hair in plaits. I watched their faces, not being able to hear them. His was the same all through his talking: earnest and asking. Hers showed first surprise, embarrassment, and pleasure, then concern as she began to nod her head. She forgot the loose wrapper she'd held so close when she first opened the door and came hurrying down the front walkway with her hands out, calling to me, "Get out! Come in!"

She had the back car door open and Jim in her arms before Dr. Joe could reach her. I can see her now hurrying up the walkway, her kimono and hair swinging loose and unnoticed. There's always a lot to say about the wicked of the world, but not much about the good except that they're good. They're rare, but they exist, for which we can be thankful.

It turned out that her brother, the Reverend Skinner, was away in Birmingham for three days for some kind of Christian Conference—I forget the name and it doesn't matter. He was pretty surprised when he came home to find us, but by then we were well settled into routine. He was used to his sister and didn't care who she brought in so long as it didn't interfere with his work and comfort, and she saw to that. That woman could have organized a thunderstorm. She was always coming and going, never hurrying after the first hour we arrived, but never idle. Even when she sat and talked to me, and she often did without making it seem like a favor, she was working at something on her lap, mending or sewing or peeling potatoes.

Dr. Joe stopped in once or twice a day, and in no time he had Jim's ears ringing with quinine. But the chills and fever were soon gone—first skipped two days instead of one, then dropped to every third and fourth and stopped. He often came with quinine in one hand and a sack of lemons in the other. Miss Verity kept a pitcher of lemonade by Jim's bed all day long. He had so much he even let me drink some. The room never lost the smell of lemons even at night. She had set up a cot for me there so I could sleep and be night nurse if it was necessary, though it wasn't after the first few days.

A week and Jim was up most of the time, but she made us stay two. He was feeble from not eating right and regular, that was the thing, or he'd have been up before. When Dr. Joe saw how we were both gaining, he began to talk about the future, not in any pressing way, just naturally. He remembered what I'd told him the first morning about Uncle Earl in Montgomery, so I embroidered on it, making out we'd be welcome and wanted, which he didn't question, being ignorant of Aunt Olive.

Miss Verity asked among her brother's congregation for clothes that would fit us, and one afternoon she and Dr. Joe made a kind of party for just the four of us, showing us the clothes and a nice suitcase Dr. Joe had found to put them in. Miss Verity had baked a coconut cake and made vanilla ice cream, like somebody's birthday, and I would have been happy except for the thought of leaving them. For his surprise Dr. Joe presented us with a neat envelope in which were bus tickets to Montgomery and a five-dollar bill.

It's a marvel how quick you can love or hate someone and never forget them. I certainly loved Verity Skinner and Joe Tatum, and in my youthful fancy had them falling in love and marrying, me having brought them together, or at least made them suddenly conscious of each other. I'm certain she did love him. I'd seen her smile when he came in the room with his lemons and quinine. I'd seen the way she watched his hands move and touch Jim. I had especially noted her voice speaking his name when he wasn't there. I'm equally certain that he saw in her only the good, busy old maid she must have appeared to all the town ever since she was no older than I. I'll bet he married a pretty ninny not worth Miss Verity's little finger, and I'll bet he was happy with her and that Miss Verity was happy for them. Not all unrequited love is tragic, or even sad. I could have written to them in later years, or gone down there easy enough to learn what had happened to them. But I never did and I never will. I don't have to know everything.

The day we left was something. It must have been around the middle of October the best I can reconstruct the passing of days, because people had begun to talk a lot about the election coming, and I remember posters at the bus station with Herbert Hoover looking embalmed and Franklin D. Roosevelt smiling like tomorrow's sunrise. Before we got on the bus Dr. Joe bought all of us milk shakes and then stuffed Jim's pockets with candy bars and gave me two packs of chewing gum, Spearmint and Juicy Fruit, and a movie magazine with Janet Gaynor on the cover. Both of them shook hands with us and said how much they'd enjoyed our staying with them. Dr. Joe told the bus driver to

take care of us. Then I lost sight of them as we settled
down in our seats.

But when the bus rolled out of the station I saw they'd
gone to the sidewalk, where they waved us off with big
smiles. A man at the back of the bus started to sing
"Happy Days Are Here Again." Another shouted, "We
want beer!" Everybody laughed and clapped and suddenly
we were gone from the town of Thebes, Alabama.

I opened my movie magazine but couldn't read it. All I
could see was Miss Verity and Dr. Joe smiling and waving
good-by. How I loved them. If only I could make them
love each other and know I'd done it so they'd love me too.
Jim said, "You look like a sick cat," and unwrapped a But-
terfinger.

CHAPTER 8

To say Aunt Olive was glad to see us would be like saying the South was glad it lost the Civil War. I think she'd have fainted if she hadn't been sustained by the horror of the moment.

The way it happened was, when we got off at the bus station in Montgomery after riding three and a half hours, it was around two o'clock. We claimed our suitcase and lugged it into the waiting room, where I changed Dr. Joe's five-dollar bill and asked the man counting it out what was the best way to get to Uncle Earl's number on South Hull Street. He said a Dime Taxi might take us quickest but then again might haul us all over Creation for an hour while it picked up and put down other passengers. I guess he just liked to talk, because then he said there was a city bus, the Cloverdale it was called, that ran right past where we wanted to go. He walked us out to the sidewalk to point and show us which corner to stand on and wait. He said the corner was important because going the way we wanted to go the bus was called the Cloverdale bus, whereas the same bus when it turned around and came back through Downtown was called the Day Street bus. I thanked him.

We paid our nickels when the bus stopped—Jim wanted to do it, so I let him, while I carried the suitcase. Seeing we were strangers, the driver was obliging, and as we went by some Downtown stores and into a traffic circle he told us this was Court Square, then that the picture show we passed was named the Strand. We headed up into Dexter Avenue, as he called it, where we rode a little before making a right turn into Hull Street. Immediately, we were out of the business district where it was just houses and went a long way in a straight line till we got there. The driver showed me which house he thought it was we wanted and didn't start his bus till we checked it by the number and I turned around to wave thank you. He waved back and pulled off, and I rang the doorbell. It played a little tune somewhere inside but nothing happened, so after waiting a minute I rang it again. Though the front windows were open, I thought they must have gone off and was about to sit down on the doorsteps and wait till they came home when I heard a voice inside I recognized as Aunt Olive's saying, "Thelma, why don't you answer that doorbell?"

A Negro woman's voice said, "Got my hands in dishwater, Miz Anderson."

"Well, you know I was lying down trying to take my nap."

Jim smirked at me.

Thelma said, "Can't help it. Nothing said about answering doorbells when I come here to help you out, just housework, and God knows there's plenty of that with them chirrun of yours leaving things everywhere and tracking my floors."

The front door opened and there stood Aunt Olive. That was when she got her shock. She caught her breath with an effort. "Lord in Heaven!" she exclaimed. "I knew it would happen!—Go right away! Shoo!" She slammed the door in my face, then opened it again slowly and stared at us like she couldn't believe her own eyes even though she'd said she "knew it would happen."

Jim picked that moment to be sociable. "Hey there, Aunt Olive," he greeted her politely.

She shifted her eyes from me to him, but her expression didn't change any for the better. "Mr. Anderson had a letter from some busybody down there named Rice saying you-all had run away and what to do. I can't imagine why she wrote us. I told Mr. Anderson not to answer that letter!"

"Yes'm," I said and decided to plunge in. "We've come to live with you like Uncle Earl said to." He hadn't said quite that, but I'd told Jim and others he had so many times I think I believed it myself.

She was outraged. "He wouldn't have dared to write such a thing to that woman!"

"I don't know, ma'am, but he sure said it to me when he came down with Mama's tombstone."

"That tombstone cost the earth, even with our business connections! I told him to mark my words he'd rue the

53

day—he'd see our children starve if he spent all his money on fripperies!"

"Well'm, he said to come and here we are."

Jim nodded confirmation, then asked me, "Is this where Mama lived when she was little?"

Aunt Olive said, "Don't go thinking that entitles *you!* This house is every penny's worth ours. Your Mama took her share in cash and threw it away on that farm your sorry father then lost." She gave a sudden look around like she was afraid neighbors could be watching, although the houses on either side weren't very close. "Come to the back door."

She closed the front door again with a final-sounding bang, so there was nothing to do but what she said. The yard was big and real nice, with trees and neat grass and a few fall flowers still blooming by a fish pond. There was one of those swing-things painted white with two seats facing each other and a slatted floor for your feet, and I wondered if it had always been there and if Mama had ever sat and swung in it. Somehow I could see her doing it. There was no back porch but the door was open because it was a warm day, so we peered through the screen at Thelma washing dishes, and she turned her head to give us a look. Aunt Olive came and unlatched the screen door, opening it a crack. Taking this as all the invitation she was likely to offer, I picked up our suitcase, but she said, "Leave that thing outside," so sharp I put it down again. Jim and I went in.

Thelma looked at us again, then turned to Aunt Olive and wanted to know, "Who they?"

"They're just nobody," Aunt Olive assured her.

"We're kinfolks," Jim piped out. "We come to live."

Thelma did not hesitate, but dried her hands on her

apron and took it right off. "Two chirrun is already two too many in a house where I work, but two more and I quit. Give me what you owe me, Miz Anderson, and I'll be on my way."

"See what you've done!" Aunt Olive accused us before giving her attention back to the unmotherly Thelma. "They're not staying, I promise you. Now, put that apron on!"

"No'm, I reckon not. My feet hurt. I needs a rest. When I take a notion to work again I let you know and if your house ain't still overrun with chirrun I might consider it."

"Thelma, you are deliberately trying my patience," Aunt Olive declared. "There's other women looking for jobs, you know!"

"Yes'm, but not so many willing to work for what you willing to pay."

"Haven't I been good to you as I could be?"

"Well'm," Thelma said, dodging a straight answer, "I'll miss the three dollars a week, don't say I won't, but I can't abide no more chirrun. Run me distracted."

"Thelma, *please* put your apron back on?—This minute!"

"Got the headache. I figure you owe me half a week. That's a dollar and a half."

"I won't pay you unless you finish those dishes!"

"Then don't look for me never again, Miz Anderson, and that's my last word!" Thelma took a black straw hat from a hook on the back door and set it on her head. Bending, she found a big brown paper sack that seemed to hold some things of hers and peered into it, then poked her hand down in it and felt around, giving Aunt Olive plenty of time to think and consider.

Aunt Olive wavered, broke. "I'll go find my pocket-book." She left the kitchen, head high.

Thelma stopped her sack poking and looked at us darkly. "We're sure enough kinfolks," I said.

"Huh," Thelma said.

"Aunt Olive is our Aunt," Jim offered.

"Huh," Thelma said.

A door banged in the front of the house and in a minute Big Britches Mister Lucien Anderson stomped his way into the kitchen, but when he saw us he stopped like he'd been struck by lightning.

"Hey there, Lucien," Jim said.

"Hey there nothing! What are you doing here?" Lucien said.

"We come to live," Jim said.

Lucien took such a deep breath I thought he'd pop, but when his face went purple he let it all out in yelling: "Mama, Mama!"

"My nerves—headaches—drive me distracted—" Thelma complained to no one, to the world, stirring a big spoonful of soda into a glass she'd poured half full of water. When it dissolved she threw her head back, holding her hat on with one hand, and drank it down.

Aunt Olive hurried in with her pocketbook. "What are you doing home, my Precious?" she said to Lucien.

"It's three o'clock," Lucien said like she was crazy. "School's out."

"Lord, where's the day gone? And where's Alice? You know you're never to leave school without her!"

"It's Wednesday—her piano lesson," Lucien said with sarcastic patience.

Aunt Olive shook her head, then nodded it. "My mind's

gone," she said, hugging herself with compassion. "They've simply put me out of my mind!"

"Miz Anderson," Thelma said, "if you'll just hand over my—"

Lucien said, "What are they doing here, Mama?"

"They're just here to—"

"Dollar and a half and we're even," Thelma finished her thought.

Aunt Olive stared at her as one waking from a dream, then unsnapped her pocketbook, found a small purse inside, and unsnapped it.

"Mama, give me a dime!" Lucien said, not to miss such an opportunity, and held out his hand.

"One dollar and fifty cents," Thelma said, "before I go out of *my* mind."

Aunt Olive counted the amount into Thelma's hand in small change of all sizes.

"I got to pee," Jim said to me. "Where's the privy?"

Thelma, who had been counting aloud, finished, "Forty-eight, forty-nine, fifty; one dollar and a half; I thank you, good-by!" She picked up her paper sack and marched out the back door, letting the screen slam.

"Country bumpkin!" Lucien jeered at Jim, and mocked him with his words, " 'Where's the privy?' —We have a bathroom, we don't use privies, but a country bumpkin like you can't use ours! Can he, Mama?"

"Are you sure Alice is all right?" Aunt Olive asked Lucien, then nodded reassurance to herself. "It *is* Wednesday. Did you wait to see her actually go through the door and tell her not to leave till you came back to get her?"

"Yes, Mama! Who's going to kidnap old Alice!"

"You never know, your father being a prominent business man."

Jim pulled at my arm. "Trudy, I got to go bad."

"Aunt Olive," I said, "you better tell us where the bathroom is unless you want an accident on your clean floor, and I'm not joking."

"Oh, my stars!" She threw up her hands. "Through there, quickly, quickly!"

I took the direction she'd indicated, with Jim at my heels, and sure enough we found the bathroom and went in together. I closed the door and stood facing away from Jim while he did it. He was so nervous he made a little splash on the floor and I told him to wipe it up with toilet paper before I flushed. Then we both rinsed our hands and dried them on the edge of a towel. It smelled nice in there, of sweet soap and talcum powder and toothpaste, and it was cool after being on buses most of the day.

Jim said almost like asking a question, "Mama lived here."

I let us stay as long as I thought we ought to because I didn't look forward to going back to the kitchen and continuing my argument with Aunt Olive and that chicken-hockey cousin of ours, but when we did go, nobody was there. I heard Aunt Olive talking to herself like, and we went to find her. She was in the living room at the front of the house and just hanging up the telephone.

"If they touch anything of mine, I'll kill 'em!" Lucien declared.

"Your father is coming right home," Aunt Olive said. "You go and get your sister. I want you both here."

"She's supposed to stay a whole hour!" Lucien complained. "I just got home. You have to pay for the whole hour whether she stays or not!"

Aunt Olive's eyes flickered but she said, "Nevertheless, go and bring her home." She opened her pocketbook again and took out a dime, handing it to Lucien. "Don't stop on the way there or back, you hear me?"

Lucien grabbed the dime and ran out the front door.

Aunt Olive stared a moment into her pocketbook before snapping it closed. "Money just evaporating since you came," she said, and began to cry.

"We got money, Aunt Olive," Jim said, bringing her attention back to us.

I kicked his foot to be quiet about that, but she ignored what he'd said and shrilled, "Don't stand there like that! Sit down somewhere. —No, not on my nice sofa. Go through into the dining room and sit on those straight chairs, and I don't want either of you to move or make a sound until Mr. Anderson comes home!"

We went through the archway into the dining room and found chairs against the wall. The room was quiet a minute until Jim, out of nervousness, or just being absentminded, began to kick his heels against the bottom bar joining the chair legs. "Don't do that!" Aunt Olive screamed, after which the two of us sat frozen maybe a quarter of an hour until Uncle Earl came.

If it hadn't been so important to us, I could have felt sorry for him when he walked in, for there she sat facing the door, Fate clutching her pocketbook in her lap, eyes like the North Pole; and there we sat, kinfolk come begging.

"You see?" Aunt Olive finally managed to say in a strangled voice.

He saw, all right, looking from her to us. If he'd put his sweaty felt hat back on his head and walked out and kept walking till he came to the Gulf of Mexico, few could have blamed him. Instead, after chewing his bottom lip for about a minute he came in to us and asked how we'd got there. I told him the bus, and that some people (without naming them) in Thebes had bought the tickets after Jim had been sick with malaria there.

Aunt Olive jumped up from her chair. "Malaria fever! Oh, my poor precious children!" she cried, not meaning us.

Uncle Earl said to her, "It's not catching, and he's over it anyway."

She said, "What if a mosquito bit him and then bit Alice and Lucien?—You see?"

As if to support her the front door opened and in came Lucien with Alice, who was wearing a starched green linen dress with white collar and cuffs that looked like it had never been sat on, or even breathed in.

"Mama," Alice said, beginning to cry in anticipation, "Lucien says I have to share my room with *her!*"

"No, never, my dearest Angel!" Aunt Olive promised her.

"I won't do it! I won't do it!" Alice blubbered, ignoring her mother's assurance. "I hate her! She can't touch my things!"

"Olive," Uncle Earl said, "will you kindly take the children some place else for a little while?"

Aunt Olive bridled. "Are you ordering your children out of their own home so that you can accommodate virtual strangers?"

That got Alice going like a cloudburst, and even Lucien, who couldn't have cried real tears at his own funeral, set up a protesting, piteous wail.

Uncle Earl came to Jim and me and herded us off into the kitchen and out the back door. Jim grabbed our suitcase as we passed it, and I wasn't sure myself that Uncle Earl wasn't just taking us to the sidewalk to point out the right corner to catch the Day Street bus to the station

Downtown. But stopping at the swing he told us to stay there while he went in to talk to Aunt Olive. He didn't try to make us welcome, nor did I expect it, but he took our suitcase with him.

Jim trotted off to the fish pond, and I followed him. After watching a few minutes we counted five good-sized goldfish. Then we went back to the swing, and its motion as we sat one on either seat showed us how to keep it going with the slightest pumping of our legs. Jim laughed, the first time I'd heard him laugh since Mama died back in May. I told him whatever happened, whether we stayed or had to leave, not to mention our money again.

He said, "How come?"

I surprised him by yelling at him, which I hadn't done for some time. "Just you mind me like I say and not ask why!" Everybody but Jim got to raise his voice that day, but that's how it is when you're the end of the line.

Uncle Earl returned after a while and told us we could come back in, so we did. It was clear from the expression on his face that Things Had Been Settled. Aunt Olive sat on the sofa in the living room with Alice on one side of her and Lucien on the other. They sat still enough to have their picture taken, but their faces looked more like waiting for the firing squad. In front of them, as I suspected Aunt Olive had made him promise to do, he explained how it was to be. I don't think I ever heard the word "temporary" used so many times in one short speech. What was "temporary," of course, was Jim and me; everybody and everything else was permanent.

We were allowed to stay with them, but it was only a "temporary" arrangement. They hadn't room for us, and besides, Uncle Earl didn't know where or how we would live after we left them, but he was going to "arrange something suitable." We would not be enrolled in school, because we were there so "temporary." Lucien had his own room, and Alice had hers, and under no circumstances were we to set foot in either. The room Jim and I were to share was the guest room. We were to consider being allowed to use it a great privilege and be careful of everything. If anything was broken, we would be punished. We were to wash and iron our own clothes and do any little jobs Aunt Olive ordered us to do. The one bathroom was downstairs, and we were not to enter it when anybody else was there, and when we did go, we were to do whatever we went for as quick as we could. I was to see that both of us came to the table clean. In addition to not going into Lucien and Alice's rooms, we were not to touch anything they said was theirs. We were to eat what we were given and not leave a scrap on our plates. We would go to bed and get up when told. We would make no noise in the guest room. "Nor in any other room!" Aunt Olive added. We were allowed to go into the yard, but not to walk off the property without "express permission." We must avoid talking to neighbors. If anybody asked us who we were, it was all right to say Gertrude and James Maynard as long as we didn't talk about being kin to the Andersons. We were not to say to anyone that we lived there, but were only making a "temporary" stop.

Jim spoke not a word during Uncle Earl's speech, and I said nothing beyond an occasional "yes, sir" to show I was taking everything in when he paused for breath. When he was done, Aunt Olive showed us the room upstairs we were to use. It was a pretty room but odd-shaped; no two walls had the same dimensions. There were two windows with ruffled white curtains, and the same material was used as a counterpane on the big bed. She left the curtains but took the counterpane off the bed and carried it with her when she went, telling us not to unpack our suitcase and ordering me to come downstairs and finish washing the dishes, since it was entirely our fault that Thelma had quit.

When she'd gone, I pushed the door to without quite closing it. Jim was wandering around examining things. There was a blue china lady's slipper on the dresser with hairpins and buttons in it. An ashtray said "Souvenir of New Orleans" on its rim. The lamp on the bedside table had a frilled blue shade, but it didn't work; only the electric light in the ceiling worked from a wall switch. Jim turned that on and off a few times until I made him stop. A pale blue bowl held a bunch of wax roses, which Jim had never seen before. I'd seen things like that because I was in and out of other people's houses in Pluma before we moved from town to country and Mama got sick and I had to stay home so much.

For no reason Jim got the giggles. I told him to shush or they'd send us away, which made him giggle harder. He tried not to make any noise, although his eyes watered with the effort. Finally I just said, "Silly," and left him to giggle by himself while I went to the kitchen. In the hall I passed Lucien's and Alice's rooms. When they heard me, both of them sprang up from their chairs and came to their doors, folding their arms, grimly guarding their treasures. Alice stuck her tongue out at me, but I ignored her, although I longed to give her a good slap.

While I finished doing the dishes, Jim came through the kitchen and went out into the back yard by himself. On going upstairs I saw that somebody had opened our suitcase on the floor and left things in a tumble. We had supper at six o'clock. Aunt Olive showed me how she wanted the table set. Supper was fried pork chops, rice and gravy, turnip greens, and strawberry Jello for dessert. Aunt Olive wasn't as good a cook as Miss Verity. After supper they all went into the living room to listen to "Amos 'n' Andy" while I washed the dishes and Jim dried. We didn't know what to do after that, so we went and stood in the doorway to the living room.

The radio was off and Uncle Earl was reading the *Alabama Journal*. Alice and Lucien were on the floor with a lot of schoolbooks spread around, doing their homework. Aunt Olive was standing with her hands under the bulb of a floor lamp cutting her fingernails. She looked over and saw us and, keeping the same frown she'd needed to concentrate on her fingernails, said, "You children can go to bed now." Uncle Earl blushed and looked like he was about to say something till she gave him a look that made him think better of it. He did manage though to call, "Good night!" when we were halfway up the stairs. Alice and Lucien hadn't looked up; nor had they spoken to us all during supper, which was just fine with me. As we got into the nightgowns Miss Verity had provided both of us, Jim whispered, "What are they going to do with us?" I shook my head, letting him take it any way he could.

CHAPTER 9

Next afternoon, when I finished washing dishes and Jim finished drying, I gave a swipe or two to the kitchen floor with Thelma's rag mop and told Jim to wait for me at the back door. First, I tiptoed upstairs and took a dollar of our money from inside my pillowcase, where I hid it during the day, and tiptoed downstairs again. Next, I went to the bathroom and flushed the toilet, having calculated it would rouse but not fully wake Aunt Olive from her afternoon nap. "I won't be sleeping if you should consult me about anything," she'd said. But I'd heard her snoring away the last half hour. I was standing at the open door of her and

Uncle Earl's bedroom across the hall from the bathroom when the toilet tank, after filling itself, began to mumble in a dove-cooing way. Aunt Olive stirred on the bed. Matching my voice to the sound of the toilet I said, "All right if we go for a little walk, me and Jim?"

"Um? Oh? Um," she said, was asleep again.

I took it as "express permission" and, finding Jim waiting where I'd told him, grabbed him by the hand and pulled him out the back door, going, "Shh!" all the time so he wouldn't show any loud surprise. At the fish pond I let him go. "Jim," I said, "how'd you like to go Downtown by ourselves and just adventure some?"

He blinked, taking it in, but caught some of my excitement, though I tried to hide it. "Yeah!" he said with his whole heart and soul. Just then we saw a bus turning into Hull Street from Cloverdale Road and ran to catch it at the corner. I had looked over Uncle Earl's *Alabama Journal* that morning after Lucien and Alice went to school and Aunt Olive went to the A&P store; and I had picked up several ideas about Montgomery. Anyway, it didn't matter what we did, because everything was new to us. We got off the bus when it turned into Dexter Avenue and walked up and had a look around the State Capitol building at the top of the hill. We took turns standing on the gold star where Jefferson Davis spoke the Oath as President of the Confederacy. Jim liked doing it even though he didn't know anything about all that, and I didn't remember enough from school to tell him; but you don't have to know much history to enjoy its leftovers. Then we went down Dexter Avenue past some rooming houses and the Grand Theater, where a company called the Mary Jane Lane Players were doing plays. Walking on, we dawdled in front of the shop windows, although I was afraid to go into any until we came to the big Kress five-and-ten-cent store. The candy counter was right by the door; the smell of candy drew us in. After looking over everything I bought us a nickel's worth of chocolate-covered peanuts. I carried the sack and doled out only a piece or two at a time. Jim said those peanuts were the best things he'd ever tasted in his life.

We walked slow, looking at everything. My eye was mainly taken with the pretty things ladies could wear. Jim lingered at the counter that had school supplies. I could tell he had his heart set on a red pencil box from the way he looked at it, but I pretended not to notice and after a minute he followed along behind me. I just didn't want to spend our money too quick.

Coming out of Kress—and we must have spent a good hour there—we walked on down by a big store called Montgomery Fair and saw the Strand Theater across Court Square. We watched the way other people crossed the square, which was really a circle, and did what they did. The picture at the Strand was *The Hatchet Man* with Edward G. Robinson. We looked at all the scenes they showed outside and I decided we just ought to go. The price was ten cents for children under twelve, and I figured with me being runty I might get away with it. The lady selling tickets didn't even ask how old I was.

Though it was the first time either one of us had been in any kind of theater, we seemed to know just what to do. I gave the tickets to a man at the door and we followed the sound into the dark auditorium. The picture was on and we sat down in the first seats we came to. It didn't matter that the picture was in the middle or that Edward G. Robinson was playing a Chinaman in San Francisco. We accepted it all and understood it all. When the picture ended, we moved down front closer to the screen. A newsreel came on and then previews of coming attractions with exploding stars and searchlights and music good enough to march to war by. Then *The Hatchet Man* was shown again, and we saw it all the way through. Jim wanted to stay on after that and see everything twice, but I realized it must be getting late and hurried us out to the corner of Dexter Avenue where the Cloverdale bus stopped.

It was turning dark when we got to Uncle Earl's and went around the house to the back door. Aunt Olive was in the kitchen cooking supper. She blessed us out when she saw us but was too busy, and too determined to have me help her, to ask many questions. That evening followed the pattern of the one before. Alice and Lucien ignored us, never saying a word to us directly, only making a few hinting, complaining remarks to their mother. Uncle Earl hadn't much to say to anybody, but I felt he might have acted all right if he hadn't been a combination of embarrassed by us and nervous of Aunt Olive.

After dessert, canned sliced peaches with Pet Milk poured over, they all trooped off to listen to "Amos 'n' Andy" while I cleaned up the kitchen with Jim helping the best he could. He was quiet, but in a different way from usual. I knew he wasn't just off in his mind by himself; he was thinking about all we'd done that afternoon.

When we got upstairs, after hesitating just a minute at the living room door to say good night, Jim said, "Can we go see *The Hatchet Man* again tomorrow?"

I told him certainly not; we had to watch our money. He undressed and pulled his nightgown on over his head and knelt down by the bed to say his prayers. Opening his eyes to look around at me as I got into my nightgown, he asked, "Do I still say, 'God bless Papa'?"

I shrugged. "Might as well."

He closed his eyes and finished saying his prayers to himself, then hopped into bed. I turned off the wall switch and found the bed in the dark. As I climbed in and settled myself Jim said, "I said, 'God bless Edward G. Robinson,' too, Trudy."

"You don't want to crowd your prayers with too many names," I cautioned him.

He turned over and went to sleep. I lay awake worrying. It was clear to me they weren't going to keep Jim if they could put him off on somebody else, yet my idea of traveling alone was based on knowing Jim would be at Uncle Earl's and taken care of. Better mean relatives than strangers you don't know anything about, was the way I thought of it.

I heard Alice and Lucien come upstairs and go to bed. I lay there, not able to sleep. A minute would seem like an hour as I listened to Jim's breathing and compared it to my own. And then I'd lose all track of time and even what I was thinking. I only knew I was bolt awake. When I thought I might be able to sleep at last, I began to get the slight itching to pee. I decided it was nothing but my imagination, and it came on stronger.

Well, there was no law against it.

I slid out of bed carefully and opened the door to the hall. The whole upper floor was quiet, but a light came up from the stairs, so I decided they must still be awake. That relieved me. I wouldn't be bothering them any. But when I was halfway down the stairs, the light in the living room went off and I heard Uncle Earl talking as he walked to the bedroom where I imagined Aunt Olive already was. "The boy will have to be a ward of the state, but the girl can work for her keep. It's possible somebody might decide to adopt the boy, he's young enough." I crept down the stairs and stood in the lower hall, knowing I had to pee before going back to bed, undecided how to get to the bathroom without causing some kind of fuss or complaint.

"Nobody's going to adopt him," Aunt Olive said. "Why would anybody want him even if they could afford it?"

I heard Uncle Earl taking off his shoes. "Well," he said, sounding sullen, "I'm doing the best I can."

"I won't be satisfied till they're out of this house," Aunt Olive said. "I don't see them put a bite in their mouths without considering how they threaten the future of our own children."

"Oh, Olive," Uncle Earl said weakly.

"You mark me," she said. I heard the bed creak and supposed she was getting into it. "I know they're your sister's, but I can't stand them. A willful mother and a weak father—it shows in both of them. The boy is plain dumb, surely you've noticed; and the girl is independent, or would be if she dared." There was another creak of the bed and the room went dark. The whole house was dark. There I was at the bottom of the stairs with my bladder full and determined not to go the bathroom lest they wonder how much of their talking I'd heard.

There was just one thing to do. My eyes were used to the dark; they'd had practice in the country. I made my mind picture everything I had to pass as I went through the dining room into the kitchen and out the back door, careful latches didn't scratch or fall nor doors bump or bang. In the yard I went a little away from the house. The grass was night-damp under my bare feet. Then I stood with my legs arched apart and peed, the way I'd seen country women do, pausing in the fields at their work and doing it as unconcerned as cattle. I'd never felt so ugly in my life. When I crept back upstairs, the whole house was sleeping. I slipped into bed and Jim changed position, turning on his side and saying something in his sleep I didn't understand. Lying there I wished I'd gone on and kept going that night I'd started to leave the farm by myself. Jim rolled over toward me and I pushed him away. "Stay on your side of the bed!" I told him, but he didn't even wake up.

CHAPTER 10

When I look back and think about it all, the thing that's hardest to grasp is the way we didn't expect any better. Things had been hard most of my life and all of Jim's, so we didn't think of times as bad but accepted them as ordinary, without feeling for one second they would ever be better.

I remember Friday as the day of Jim and the goldfish. To this minute I'm not sure I know what possessed him. In a way it was like him to do the very wrong thing when he was trying to help. Then too, he was a country child, and country children think of fish as fish, not something pretty to look at. Back of it must have been Aunt Olive's complaining. She kept up a running conversation with herself all day about how much food cost, and how much more she was having to spend on it with us there with them. She was sure her own children would be forced into the streets to beg if "other arrangements" were not made about us soon. None of us, she declared, could be certain of the next meal.

Children tend to believe what they hear. —Not Lucien and Alice, because they were used to their mama; but I think Jim took every word Aunt Olive uttered as Gospel truth.

Uncle Earl drove home for noon dinner as usual. Aunt Olive said she'd drive him back to his office because she wanted to ride around and visit friends during the afternoon. In front of the three of us at the dinner table—Alice and Lucien had a "lunch period" at school—she said she just had to get away for an hour "from everything."

I washed the dishes with Jim helping. He liked everybody being gone but us and said we ought to lock the doors and not let them in when they came back. I laughed along with him, which encouraged him to propose we go down to the Strand after we finished and see *The Hatchet Man* again. I wouldn't let us, but told him to go out in the yard while I washed a few of our things and put them to dry. About an hour later, when I was hanging clothes, I saw him swinging himself and sort of singing or humming.

Upstairs I decided it wouldn't hurt anybody if I looked at Alice's room. I didn't have to go inside but opened the door and craned my neck around. It was beautiful. There was wallpaper with roses on it, pretty enough for a living room. There was a four-poster bed with a white counterpane fringed at the bottom. Alice had her own dainty desk and dresser and a soft-looking chair to sit in. Her curtains were white like the counterpane, and being Alice's everything was clean and neat as a pin. I closed the door the way I'd found it and decided to go sit in the living room while everybody was out and look through *Liberty* magazine and the *Reader's Digest* that were kept out on what they called the library table, although I hadn't seen a single book in the house, except schoolbooks, not even a Bible.

I had settled down to read a story in *Liberty* when I heard a scream that brought me to my feet. I didn't even recognize Aunt Olive's voice, but went running toward the sound outdoors. Jim had taken his shoes and socks off and was in the fish pond. At first I thought that was all. Then I saw on the lawn near the pond two big goldfish he'd managed to catch and throw out with his hands, they being so tame and lazy. And there was Aunt Olive a few yards away from him where she'd stopped, screaming her head off.

"Come out of there this minute!" Those were the first real words she managed to say.

He climbed over the side, and she was waiting for him. She gave him one slap after another, and he commenced to cry as I ran to pull him away from her.

"I'll make Earl wear you out with his belt!" she threatened as Jim bawled and I tried to hold myself between them. She pushed me aside and gave him another slap, demanding to know, "Why did you do it?"

"I caught them for supper!" he cried. I took him by the arms and shook him, but not hard, only wanting him to stop crying in front of Aunt Olive.

"Look what you've done!" She pointed to the fish on the grass. "They're dead! You've killed them!" Sure enough there wasn't a twitch or wiggle in them; they just lay there.

"You're a wicked, ungrateful child, and it won't surprise me if you wind up in the electric chair!" She made for him again, but I was between them, and I stayed between them.

"Jim," I said, "go upstairs." He ran to the kitchen door.

"When did you start giving orders in my house, missy?" she said. —"Get your hands off me!" I was only trying to restrain her until she got calm. "I'm telling your uncle you fought back at me, you see if I don't!"

And, of course, she did.

But first Lucien and Alice came home from school and had to be told what had happened. Alice set up a howl that would have drowned a locomotive; a stranger would have thought those fish were her best friends. Lucien asked if he could skin and stuff them. He'd sent away for some kind of mail-order course in that kind of thing. Alice cried louder, and while Aunt Olive tried to comfort her, Lucien took the fish off toward the garage, where he kept what he called his laboratory. Aunt Olive got Alice into the house and up to her room, and I went to see about Jim in the guest room. He was sitting on the floor with his arms around his knees, like he was afraid to touch anything, and more: just afraid. I didn't know what to say, so I didn't say anything, but got myself busy darning a shirt collar he'd chewed absentmindedly the last time he wore it, just to show I didn't think anything so almighty awful had happened.

Alice had stopped crying and was telling her mama about a party she'd been invited to by one of the girls at school who had a birthday coming up. The girl's name was Fanny-Maude, and Fanny-Maude was going to invite seven girls and eight boys. Alice and her mama started talking about what she would wear, and you wouldn't have known either of them had been upset about anything half an hour earlier.

Uncle Earl came home complaining that he'd had to take the bus because Aunt Olive hadn't come to get him like she said she would, and that got everything back to Jim and the goldfish. Jim and I stayed upstairs but we could hear them talking in the living room. Nobody thought of whispering when it concerned us. Uncle Earl's big news was that Jim and I were going into a Home on Monday. It was all settled.

That took the wind out of Aunt Olive's sails. "Well!" was all she could say at first, but recovered enough to add, "Now I can get Thelma to come back."

CHAPTER 11

Saturday, it poured rain.

That didn't matter to Alice, who only felt safe indoors. She had a born little-lady's distrust of any place without walls and a roof. When Jim and I finished the breakfast dishes, we didn't know what to do with ourselves. I left him standing at the kitchen door looking out and went upstairs to finish tidying the guest room. I'd already made up the bed.

Alice had her door open, and I thought she was talking to her mama until I realized she was talking to herself, something she'd picked up from Aunt Olive, I doubt not.

She's taken all her dresses from the closet and spread them on the bed and over the chair and even the desk. All shades of yellow and green and pink, polka dots and flower patterns—there seemed a hundred dresses, and probably were eight or ten.

"Now, which shall I wear to the birthday party?" she asked herself with a finger on the dimple of her chin. "The pink with white collar and cuffs?" She picked it up and studied it critically. I had paused in the hall to watch her and was about to go on when I realized she knew I was there but was pretending not to know; her talking was now for me. "No, not the pink." Back on the bed it went, and she picked up another and posed it against herself in front of the dresser mirror. "Green polka dot is pretty and I've worn it only once, but mean Lucien says I look freckled in it." As she examined another I saw her take a sly glance at me in the mirror. "It will be *so* nice to have our house all to ourselves again, just Mama and Daddy and Lucien and me. How I long for Monday." She stamped her foot. "Naturally, I can't ask anybody I know to come see me while *they're* here! I don't think people ought to go where they're not welcome and wanted. I know very well *I* wouldn't!" She pretended to discover me and wheeled around. "Are you spying on me? Well, since you are, which do you think is prettiest?" Her eyes were beady with spite. "I've got so many I can't make up my mind."

I didn't answer her, but went on to the guest room. While I was tidying, Aunt Olive called me from downstairs. I found her in the kitchen wearing a rain coat and carrying an umbrella. Jim was still at the back door, but they were pretending not to see each other.

"I'm going to the A&P to do the weekend shopping. You and your brother must keep out of everybody's way while

I'm gone. Alice is busy in her room, and your uncle is in the living room working on some insurance papers. You'll not disturb him if you know what's good for you. You and the boy can stay in the guest room, or if you must be downstairs, sit in the dining room. Where's Lucien?"

"Here I am, Mama!" he answered, coming in from the hall. "Where you going? Can I go with you?"

"A&P."

"Can I *go?*"

"If you do, you'll have to help carry."

"I think I'll do experiments in my laboratory."

"Don't get wet going to the garage. All I need is for my precious children to come down sick."

"I'll go under your umbrella when you get the car out."

"Well, come on."

Jim surprised me by asking if he could go with Lucien and got two loud nos from Aunt Olive and Lucien and nothing from me. Off to the garage went mother and child, sharing the umbrella so both of them got wet on one side. I told Jim to let's go sit in the dining room and look through Aunt Olive's Memory Book, but he didn't want to, so I left him staring out the door again as Aunt Olive backed down the driveway.

I found the Memory Book where it always lay on a low shelf of the sideboard. It was full of family pictures, more of Alice than anybody else. In every one she was squinting what she thought was a smile into the sun. People taking pictures then usually stood with the sun behind them. There were a few programs of school plays and things like that, and a program of a piano recital Alice had played in. Her piece was called "Over the Candy Counter." In a health pageant Lucien had played a bottle of milk. There were pictures of people I didn't know and took to be members of Aunt Olive's side of the family. One of the women looked a lot like her. She was wearing her hair bobbed and fluffed out on the sides, and her dress looked funny, so it couldn't have been a very recent picture.

I wasn't all that interested, because the pictures were either of people I didn't know or didn't care for. I had started to yawn when I heard the back door slam and in came Jim with his hair and clothes damp. "Where've you been?" I asked him.

"To the garage," he said.

"Did you wipe your feet good?"

"Yes."

"They told you not to go to the garage."

"They said I couldn't go with Lucien," he corrected me.

"Well, you know what they meant."

"I went in and saw Lucien in his old laboratory. He had my goldfish on a board, but he wasn't doing anything with them."

"What was he doing?" I said, idly turning a page of the Memory Book.

"He had his peter out playing with it."

"James Maynard! Don't you talk dirty!"

"Well, he did."

"I don't want to hear another word. —Did he see you?"

Jim nodded. "He picked up a bottle and threw it at me."

"Well, anyway," I said, "he won't likely tell on you for going to the garage. Come help me look at this book."

He pulled one of the big straight chairs over to mine and sat down, but as I turned the pages I could tell he wasn't any more interested than I was. "Are you going with me to that Orphans' Home like they said last night?"

He'd caught me by surprise again. "Well, they said so, didn't they?"

"Will they let us sleep together?"

I shook my head. "They put all the girls together and all the boys together."

"I'd sure hate to sleep with a lot of dirty orphans and not have enough to eat."

"Oh," I said, "this place is probably different. Uncle Earl wouldn't send us there unless it was all right."

"Huh," he said.

I hadn't talked to him about it last night, although he'd tried to get me to. Not able to avoid it now, I tried to encourage him to like the idea. "You'll get on all right, Jim. People will probably like you."

"Aunt Olive doesn't like me, does she?"

"My guess is you'll get along just fine and start school and be smart; and I bet pretty soon some nice family will come out there and see you and adopt you. They'll probably be rich and buy you a lot of things, and you won't ever have to think about being hungry or sleeping with other children. I won't be able to call you 'Orphan Jim' then, will I?" I nudged him to show I was joking.

He was quiet for a few minutes as I turned pages, pretending to be interested. "Look at this. Alice was a little old thing then, wasn't she?"

"What are you going to do if somebody adopts me?" Jim asked.

"We'll hoe that row when the grass grows," I told him.

"I know what you'll do—you won't even be there, that's what you'll do!"

"You're talking foolishness!" I said, and slammed the book to. "Where you going now?" He didn't answer but went into the hall, and I let him alone, because I didn't know what to say to him. The truth was that I didn't know what to do. Just because he thought I did, didn't make it so.

I put the Memory Book away and was just sitting there in the dining room by myself feeling dull. Alice drifted through from upstairs, but we didn't pay any attention to each other. I was wishing I had something to do when I heard Alice shriek and went to find out what was the matter. Uncle Earl beat me there. He was outside the bathroom shaking Jim and hitting him about the face. Alice was inside pulling her bloomers up and making a lot of noise, which was a thing Alice was good at.

"He came in while I was on the seat!" she whined.

"The door wasn't closed!" Jim protested.

"It was so!" she claimed.

"It was not!"

"Did he touch you?" Uncle Earl asked Alice. "Did he come up close? Did he *see* you?"

"I was so scared I don't know!" she wept.

Uncle Earl gave Jim another hard slap, and Jim's nose started to bleed. "I should have whipped you last night! Your aunt begged me to! Sneaky, sinful boy! —Are you all right, Alice? Are you *sure* you're all right?" When he turned to see about her, I pulled Jim back from the danger zone and along the hall. He wasn't crying; I was proud of him for that. Things would have quieted down if Aunt Olive hadn't chosen that very minute to come back with her groceries.

It had to be told. There were fresh buckets of tears from Alice. The noise everybody was making brought Lucien from the garage. The amount of shock and outrage expressed would have been justified only if Alice had been scalped and raped by a party of raiding Indians. Jim's nose stopped bleeding when I took him to the kitchen sink and washed his face. "The door wasn't closed, Trudy," he said. "Why would I go in if it was?" I believed him.

For punishment Jim was made to go out and stay in the garage the rest of the day with orders not to touch the car or go into Lucien's laboratory or turn on the electric light. He was not to eat in the dining room again either, Aunt Olive said, lest he embarrass Alice. I asked her if it was all right if I ate with him at the kitchen table. She looked relieved and nodded, not thinking, I'm sure, what a relief it was to us not to have to eat with them.

After noon dinner Jim and I washed up as usual and I walked him out to the garage. The rain had slackened, but it was dark and damp in the garage and smelled of must. I found a stack of old *Liberty* magazines, and Jim settled himself near the open door so he could look at the illustrations by daylight. I stayed on a little while, and then I went back into the house. Uncle Earl was in the living room reading the Montgomery *Advertiser*. Aunt Olive was in their bedroom taking a nap. Alice was in the dining room studying pictures of herself in the Memory Book. So I went on upstairs, not wanting to sit in the kitchen, which was the only other place I was allowed, because it smelled of dishrags that wouldn't dry.

Opening the door to the guest room, I caught Lucien at it red-handed. He had emptied our suitcase on the floor and pulled out all the drawers of the dresser, which we hadn't used because we'd been told not to. When I saw him, he was reaching his hand into my pillowcase and pulling out the money I'd hidden.

I didn't even think, I just ran, and he commenced hollering even before I got to him. Dollar bills and coins flew through the air. I don't know what I did. I certainly didn't have time to hurt him as much as he claimed, because

Aunt Olive and Uncle Earl and good old Alice were there as quick as they could move. Lucien was rescued, and I didn't hear anything said then or later about his coming into the guest room and snooping through our things.

At first I was accused of having stolen the money from them, but when they'd checked their pocketbooks and wallets and found nothing missing—and they were the kind to know to a penny what they had every minute of their lives—they accused me of stealing it before I came to their house. They wouldn't listen to my true explanation, even when I gave Dr. Joe Tatum's name and dared them to ask him. ("What! A long-distance telephone call? Will you listen to how she's willing to spend our money?") No, the money was stolen, and I must learn that people who stole did not benefit by ill-gotten gains. Therefore, since I would not reveal who I had actually stolen it from, they would keep the money. It would, Aunt Olive said, go a very little way toward paying for the enormous amounts of food we were consuming. In olden times, she said, thieves had their hands cut off.

Then Uncle Earl backed the car out and drove Lucien and Alice Downtown to a picture show. I'd heard them begging to go earlier at the dining table, but they'd been turned down. Now it was decided that they must be kept away from Jim and me as much as possible. They left arguing. Lucien wanted to go to the Tivoli to see a Buck Jones Western; Alice wanted to see Jeanette MacDonald and Maurice Chevalier in *Love Me Tonight* at the Strand; and Uncle Earl said they had to go to the same one because Lucien had to take care of his sister. Alice said there were rats in the Tivoli, which settled it. Jim and I had seen the coming attractions of *Love Me Tonight*. It looked pretty good except that people sang.

After they left Aunt Olive sat me down in the kitchen and gave me what she called a talking-to for my own good. According to her, I was vicious beyond redemption and should be sent to a reform school instead of the nice Orphans' Home Uncle Earl had persuaded to take us in, purely through his business connections. She was of a mind to discuss it with him seriously when he came home and while her precious children were safely out of the house. She was willing, if necessary, to testify to examples of my violent and vicious behavior to the authorities. I would, of course, come to no good end. If I had one ounce of decency in me, I should rejoice that Mama was not alive to see how low-down I was.

Jim and I were to stay in the garage or the guest room the rest of the time we were in their house, she said. We were not to use the bathroom at all. She would supply a pot which I would be escorted into the bathroom by her *and her alone* to empty when it became necessary. We might wash our faces and hands under the back yard spigot used to connect the hose to water the lawn. We were not to speak to anyone except each other, and as little as possible to each other. When we left on Monday, she hoped never more to set eyes on either of us. I held my tongue and sat still before her.

They're wrong who say time mutes all feelings. I've never been one to forgive; I leave it to those who enjoy it. I hated Aunt Olive then. I don't think of her often, but when I do, I hate her still.

She finally let me go upstairs. Getting down on hands and knees I went over every inch of the floor. I found two dimes and three nickels under the bed where they'd rolled. Knotting them into the corner of a handkerchief, I pinned the handkerchief to the elastic band of my bloomers. Then I stood at one of the windows a long time, looking out at the old pecan tree in the rain and trying to decide what to do.

CHAPTER 12

I didn't tell Jim what I'd decided, partly because I didn't know how it was going to happen, and partly because I wasn't sure he wouldn't let it out, if no other way, by the expression on his face. Sunday was as sunny as Saturday had been rainy, and Aunt Olive started it by telling Uncle Earl and her precious children that they were all going to Sunday School and church. (There was no question of our going, of course.) Uncle Earl always went to church because it was good for business. Alice didn't mind; it gave her a chance to dress up and see her friends. But Lucien begged to stay home. They wouldn't let him though, because Aunt Olive said she was afraid Jim and I would gang up against him. So they dressed and primped, and complained about each other's spending too much time in the bathroom, and couldn't find their Bibles and ran around like chickens with their heads cut off until they *did* find them. It seemed they scored points in Sunday School for bringing them. Each had his or her own Bible, and they kept them in drawers. Finally, after Alice must have asked fifty times how she looked, they all piled out of the house and into the car and off they drove.

Aunt Olive had given me working orders: when to light the gas oven and put in the hen and dressing she'd fixed, when to peel the sweet potatoes and set them on the stove to boil, and all the rest. She'd arranged things on the kitchen table with strict directions on exact amounts to be used. I nodded meekly to everything she told me, satisfied to know I'd never do any of it.

As soon as I was sure they'd gone—and I watched through the front window a full five minutes to make sure they didn't turn around and come back for something they'd forgot—I grabbed hold of Jim and swung him all around the room, both of us in high glee, me from relief at their going, and Jim because he was so surprised at me.

"We're going somewhere too, Jim!" I told him, letting him go.

"We're not going to the Orphans' Home!" he crowed, picking himself up from the floor. "I knew you'd think of something!"

"I haven't thought what we *will* do, only what we won't. Are you game to just *go*?"

"*Anywhere* except the Orphans' Home!"

"Come on then. Let's get our things."

I'd replaced the contents of the suitcase after Lucien had

scattered them all over the floor, so there was no packing to do. Both of us put on our heaviest clothes, because they were easier to wear than carry, and we were ready to leave fifteen minutes after the family had driven off. I don't know why, except habit I guess, but we left by the back door. I took nothing from the kitchen. Aunt Olive wasn't one to have leftover food anyway. She cooked skimpy, and everything was eaten. It was, however, a pleasure to look at the things she'd set out on the table for me to do and know she'd find them exactly the way she'd left them when she came back from worshiping the Lord.

When we went by the fish pond, Jim stopped and spat in it. "I hope they're all floating belly up the next time she looks."

We didn't have to wait long at the corner for the Day Street bus, although they didn't run so often on Sunday. By accident, the driver was the same one who'd brought us out from the bus station last Wednesday, and he remembered us. "Going traveling again?" he asked.

"All the way to the end of your run," I said. "Where's that?"

"Day Street, like it says on the front." He looked doubtful. "You sure you know where you want to go?"

"Yes, sir," I said. "Day Street."

"That's the big Nigra district; do you know that?" he asked.

I didn't. "Oh, yes, sir," I said. "We're not going to stay there. We're just passing through and leaving a message with my aunt's hired woman."

That seemed to partially satisfy him, if not entirely. I shoved Jim along to the middle of the bus so we wouldn't be close enough to the driver to talk.

As we went through the residential district, white people

got on the bus and filled it from front to back. Colored people who got on filled it from back to front, although there was no strict dividing line set; it shifted with how many colored and white were riding. By the time we'd climbed the hill of Montgomery Street to Five Points and turned off Mobile Street into Day Street, Jim and I were the only white people and had to move all the way up front. Most of the colored people had got on Downtown, and the more of them got on, the jollier they became. Just about everybody was laughing and talking by the time we turned into Day Street, which stretched out straight and long ahead of us.

I hadn't planned farther than the bus; my notion had been just to get us away from the house on Hull Street. But now as the passengers began to get off and no new ones got on, I grew nervous, because I guessed we were getting near the end of the line, and I could see the driver glancing at me in his mirror.

Most of what we passed on Day Street was houses, shacky built and weathered gray, with droopy flowers planted in old coffee cans on steps or porches. On the right we came to what looked like a schoolhouse with a hard dirt playground in front; across the street from it was a church. A little farther there were a few stores bunched together at the top of a hill, and a place with a sign that said Callie's Cafe. Across from it was what called itself Weaver's Market on the Coca-Cola advertising sign in front. The bus stopped there, and everybody got off but us, so I took the suitcase and told Jim, "Come on."

The driver twisted in his seat to look at us. I tried to give him a smile, but from his expression it didn't go too well. "This the end of the line?" I asked him.

"You might say. I go another two blocks. What's this woman's name you're looking for?"

"Thelma." I was ready for that much.

"Thelma what?" I felt a fool for not having thought of a last name for her. "You know where she lives?"

"She doesn't live on Day Street, just off it, Aunt said."

"You're looking for this Thelma, works for your aunt on Hull Street. Uh-huh." He wasn't pretending to believe me now. "I been driving this bus a long time and I've come to know a lot of cooks and maids that live out here and work in Cloverdale, because they ride my bus twice a day. But I don't seem to recollect this Thelma getting on or off where you got on today."

"She hasn't been working this week."

"You chillun are running away, ain't you?"

I knew it wasn't any use trying to fool him. "Please, mister," I said. "They didn't want us. They were going to put us in the Orphans' Home tomorrow. We dreaded to go there, so when they all went off to Sunday School this morning, we decided—"

He had started shaking his head. "Don't tell me your troubles and don't tell me your names. Just get off my bus."

"Yes, sir." I pushed Jim to hurry us down the step. "Thank you for the ride."

"Don't thank me. You paid."

On the sidewalk I turned around. He wasn't looking at us, just looking ahead at nothing, frowning. "Mister," I said, "if anybody asks if you saw us, say no, please-sir."

He let his breath out like he was exasperated. "Listen, girl. If they don't want you, like you told me and I believe, I guarantee they won't be looking for you and they won't

be asking me any questions. Come back in here a minute."
When I hesitated, he said impatiently, "Put your suitcase
down and come in for a second; it won't run away." I gave
the suitcase to Jim and stepped back on the bus. The driver
pointed ahead through the front glass. "Straight on about
half a mile a road curves off to the right and leads eventually into Bell Street. That leads eventually out of town past
Maxwell Field, big Air Force base, on to Birmingham. You
heard of Birmingham?" I nodded. "Steel and coal mining.
It's a big city compared to Montgomery. You might even
find yourself something to do there, some kind of work.
Weekdays there's a lot of trucks and you could catch a ride,
but not on Sunday." He paused, rubbed his chin, and studied about it. "You be better off waiting till tomorrow. Go
into Mr. Weaver's store and buy something to eat to carry
with you, cheese and crackers, something like that. Then
go on down Day Street till it turns off and you'll see a lumberyard. Don't be scared; the niggers won't bother you.
You could maybe stay in the lumberyard tonight so you'll
be out of the weather, get a fresh start tomorrow morning."
Finished, he looked directly at me and frowned hard.
"That's the best I can offer."

"Mister, you've been real nice to us, and I'm going to do
just like you said!"

"Just get off my bus," he said, so I did, and he drove off.

The sidewalk both sides of Day Street was crowded with
Negroes, mostly men but some women and children too.
I'd never seen so many Negroes all at one time. They were
mainly dressed in clean and what looked like best clothes.
Some were going in and out of the stores and cafe, but
most of them were idling around in twos and threes or
more, laughing and talking. I'd never seen people look so

cheerful on a Sunday, but I reckoned it didn't take much to give them a good time.

They looked at us, but no special way, as we walked into the store called Weaver's Market. The clerks were all white and wore big aprons that were messed with dirt and blood, but everybody looked cheerful in there too. The shelves were packed with groceries, and the meat case was full. A radio somewhere was tuned to a religious program called "Big Brothers' Bible Class." Flies swarmed around a counter where they sold fish.

"Step right up and get your mullet fish!" the clerk back of the counter shouted at nobody. "Five cents a pound, one nickel! Mullet fish going fast!" He was wrapping a sale he'd just made in old newspaper, and the fat Negro woman waiting for the fish shook with laughter, keeping her mouth carefully closed to hold in her dip of snuff.

Another clerk stepped up to me and said, "Something I can do for you, Young Lady?"

That was the first time in my life anybody had called me "lady" and it made me feel good. That's probably what led me to say, "Why yes, my brother Jim and I would like a cold drink, I believe." I was sorry right away, remembering that after paying our bus fares we had only a quarter left, but he had opened the cold-drinks box.

"What'll you have, Jim?" the man said, and, after giving me a quick look to make sure it was all right, Jim said, "Orange Crush."

I had a chocolate drink. "Something else I can get for you-all, let me know." I gave him a dime; he squeezed Jim's shoulder and went on his business. We looked around between swallows from our bottles. It was a comfortable, busy, but easygoing kind of store, not like any I'd ever been in. Customers came and went, mostly buying a nickel or a

dime's worth of things like rice or sugar or coffee, loose cigarettes for a penny each, penny candy bars and such, so I
felt right at home with the fifteen cents I had left of Dr.
Joe's money.

Back of the meat counter the butcher was cutting pork
chops for a Negro couple. The man and woman watched
him soberly. When he turned his head, without pausing in
his work, to say something to the boy helping him, he cut a
gash in the heel of his hand, and the blood spurted. The
woman said, "Don't you bleed on my pork chops!"

"Let him," the man beside him said. "Be the only fresh
thing about that meat."

The butcher managed to keep on working and wrap a
handkerchief around his hand at the same time. Throwing
the chops on the scales he laughed and said, "You know
that ain't so, Riff. Fresh as spring water and tender as a
mother's love. The five come to twenty-two cents. What
else can I get for y'all?"

Jim finished his Orange Crush and sucked on the end of
the bottle till I told him to stop and put it in a slot in the
empty case under the icebox. I made my drink last because
I was kind of enjoying everything going on in the store. Everybody was so easy, making the most common things they
did look like having fun.

When the rush of customers was over, I bought a dime's
worth of cheese and a nickel box of saltine crackers, and we
went on our way, not wanting to invite curiosity by hanging around.

Like the bus driver had said, nobody paid any attention
to us as we walked down Day Street. The pavement ended
a couple of blocks beyond the stores, and just before it did
there was a bunch of Negro boys about my age doing some
fancy roller-skating in the street. All their movements had a

kind of free-flow gracefulness that looked almost out of control until they'd do a sudden stop and show how much in control of the skates they really were. We stood and watched them, and they put on a special show-off show.

We found the lumberyard easy enough. Nobody was around, it being a Sunday, of course. There was an office-looking low building with a padlock on the front door and stacks of lumber everywhere. There were no fences. It smelled good, of tar and resin. Jim and I settled ourselves in a sunny place. He wanted to eat, but I made us wait till it began to turn dark. By then we were so hungry, not having had anything since breakfast except the cold drinks, I didn't have the heart to save anything back for tomorrow. Maybe we'd get a ride with somebody like Bud.

When I saw the man, I had a feeling he'd been watching us a long time. Surely he must have been watching while we ate. He wasn't far away, maybe thirty feet, leaning against a stack of lumber. He was a white man. His pants were baggy. He wore a faded red sweater and a shapeless hat. He was thin; his eyes were bright and intent even in the fading daylight. He could have been any age; all I could tell was he was grown.

When I went still, he knew I'd seen him, and called, "What you chillun doing here?"

"We're not bothering anything, mister," I said, making the natural but wrong assumption that all grown men were some kind of authority.

"Who're you with?"

That should have warned me. "Nobody. By ourselves," I answered.

He looked around quickly before he came over, not hurrying exactly, but very deliberate. He ignored Jim when he got to us and took hold of me by the wrist. "Come on," he said. "I got something to show you."

I said, "No, sir. I want to stay here."

He pulled me after him. Jim didn't know what to do except follow. Later, I could think what might have saved us, but when it started happening it was a surprise, and by the time I saw what was going to be, it was too late to tell Jim to run and bring the first person he saw. Anyway, he probably wouldn't have found anybody; nor do I think he'd have left me like that.

I resisted being pulled along by the man, and Jim commenced to whimper. Fear made him bold as he'd never been with a grown-up before. "Stop holding my sister!" he demanded, but the man paid no attention.

I knew what he was going to do when he told me to shut Jim up if I knew what was good for us. By then he had me, and Jim with us, inside the V made by the two stacks of planks higher than our heads. Throwing me on the ground, he held me down with one arm and a knee while he loosened his pants and got his thing out.

"Jim! Run get somebody!" was all I was able to yell. The man was on top of me, and hard as I fought I couldn't keep him from getting in me. Jim was crying and hitting and kicking the man, who paid no more attention than if he'd been buzzed by a fly. It was over quick, that part of it. The man just sprawled out suddenly like he'd been shot, and when I kept fighting and Jim kept hitting him on the back, he rolled off and looked at me with his bright eyes like he hated me, like I'd done the bad thing to him. That scared me even more than I'd been before. I tried to crawl out of his reach, but he grabbed me by the ankle and started hitting me. Jim kept up a steady kicking and screaming, but the man slapped and hit me until I couldn't see. He didn't say a word or utter a sound. But when he'd done with me, he grabbed Jim and beat him too. I couldn't do a thing to help, just lay there wishing I was dead. I don't remember how he left or when. I only know that finally he wasn't there any more.

Jim had stopped crying. I must have had my eyes closed, for he said, "Are you dead, Trudy?"

"No."

"He's gone," Jim said.

"Did he hurt you?"

"Yes. I couldn't stop him, Trudy."

"I know it," I said, and sat up on the ground.

Jim looked like he didn't know whether to touch me or not. Then he reached his hand out and began to pat me just the way he'd patted Mama's gravestone the day we left the farm.

I sat there for a while and let Jim pat me. I felt sore all over, the way my feet were so sore after a long day's walking I could hardly bear to touch the soles. I felt dirty the way I did once when I was cleaning a chicken and the guts broke and oozed over my hands. I washed and washed my hands, but I knew they'd never be clean again. When I looked directly at Jim, his face showed sympathy and disgust. I got up from the ground and we went back where we'd been earlier to find our suitcase.

"Where we going, Trudy?" Jim asked.

"I don't know. Let's just leave here."

Out on the road we walked until we came to a crossing that had a billboard with big pictures on it of Franklin D. Roosevelt and Mr. John Nance Garner. Over the pictures were the words: Vote For. That seemed as good a place as we were likely to find, so I said, "Let's stay back of that sign tonight," and we did.

We slept on the ground with our clothes on. I woke up in the middle of the night cold, and was surprised to find I had my arms around Jim. I well remember what a shock it was.

CHAPTER 13

I cried off and on all next day. It was as though everything since Mama died had caught up with me. For a while Jim stood around looking sorry for me, but finally got bored and wandered off by himself. I let him go, then wondered what he'd do and got up to see. He only went to a filling station a hundred yards away that had been closed yesterday. When he came back, he had our old kitchen cup about half full of water. Handing it to me, he said, "If you're going to cry, you need it." He was serious, not making fun of me, so I drank it. "It was full when I started."

"I thank you."

"Want me to go get you some more?"

"No." I started crying again, and he looked at me like I had gone crazy. He let me alone though, and sat in front of the billboard to watch the cars and trucks go by. I opened the suitcase and sorted through our things. I was dry-eyed and empty-feeling till I came upon Mama's tortoise comb, and that got me going again. I was as bad as Alice.

It went on all day. Jim came back to ask weren't we going to try to hitch a ride to Birmingham. Without knowing I'd thought about it, I found myself answering, "No, we're not. This was Mama's home town and we have as much right here as anybody."

"Well," he said, "are we just going to live here back of this sign?"

"Don't be foolish," I told him.

"Trudy, I'm hungry," he said as if he was but was ashamed to say so.

"I'm not," I said, and for a wonder I wasn't.

Late in the afternoon Jim went back to the filling station to drink water and bring me some, but otherwise nothing passed into us that day. I knew I had to move sometime, but I wasn't ready. I couldn't explain it to Jim; I didn't understand it myself. Part of it was that I didn't want anybody to see me, not *anybody*. I felt that whoever did would know exactly what had happened to me.

Hunger, though, is like a separate muscle; it'll get you moving every time. Both of us woke next morning before daylight, aching cold and hungry as we'd never been. When light came, it was gray, and the sky looked like it was going to rain. We didn't talk to each other; there wasn't anything to say. I didn't have even the beginning of a plan in my head. When I picked up the suitcase, Jim walked beside me from habit. Back to Day Street we headed. It was the only place I knew other than Hull Street, and I wasn't about to lead us there.

Smoke was coming from chimneys. People walked and talked in the houses. Men set off to work. The women who worked in Cloverdale would already have caught their buses, I reckoned. Children were getting ready for school, calling things like, "Mama, can I wear my new sweater?" —"Mama, where's my spelling book you let Teresa play with last night?" The whole street was busy, but different-busy from the way we'd seen it on Sunday. This was Tuesday, and people were well into the work and school week. Tuesday is the worst day of the week for those who mind what they do. Nobody likes Monday, even Monday's mother, but Monday's over, and it's too early to believe Saturday will ever come, so people grit their teeth and go to work.

But we had nothing to do and nowhere to go. Freedom and independence are important when you haven't got them, but when they're all you've got, they're useless. There I was walking along free and independent, hard and proud in my hunger and hate, but I know that if any tyrant had spoken a gentle word to me, I'd have died of love and gratitude.

No one paid the slightest attention to us. I thought about what to do as we walked along, and decided no, I couldn't beg from Negroes. I thought of going to Weaver's Market; I couldn't. I was too proud to do either, but pride soon loses to hunger.

Telling Jim to wait with the suitcase, I went around a house I'd picked because it looked more prosperous than most of the others. It had shades on the windows, and chairs on its front porch, and plants in clay flower pots instead of coffee cans. I knocked on the back door; a middle-aged woman opened it and peered at me.

"I'm hungry. My brother and I. Could you please spare—"

She broke in. "I can spare nothing. Go beg from white folks." She slammed the door, and I went back to find Jim waiting. Coming to him alone, I saw him clear for the first time since we left Hull Street. He was dirty, his hair was tangled. His clothes showed plainly he'd not been out of them for two days and two nights. There were bruises on his face in addition to dirt, and a cut on his cheek below his right eye. The eye was smudged around with purple. I figured I looked no better.

Just as I got to him a group of schoolgirls all ages trooped by. They stopped and stared at us, then giggled and nudged each other and went on up Day Street. I don't know why, but we followed them, probably because they were children and we didn't have to be afraid of them. We went past Callie's Cafe and Weaver's Market. From there Day Street sloped downhill to the school and the church I'd noticed on Sunday.

When the children came in sight of the school, they commenced to run. I couldn't let them go. "Hey! Hey, stop!" I must have hollered loud in my desperation, because they halted at once and turned around to see what I wanted. I swallowed hard. "Do you-all know anybody'd give us something to eat?"

They looked at each other dumbfounded. The biggest girl, the one who had started the nudging and giggling back there, stepped forward. "You see that house yonder?" She pointed to a white house on a side lane just off Day Street. "Go knock on her door." The other children looked scandalized and whispered among themselves. The big girl put her hands on her hips and strutted a few steps. "Knock on the Whore's door!" Then all, as if that was a signal, broke and ran giggling into the schoolyard.

I'd have done anything anybody suggested. Taking the suitcase in one hand and Jim's hand in my other, I marched to the white house and up the front steps. Setting the suitcase down I knocked.

After a minute the door started to open, and before she saw us a woman's voice said, "I thought you was gone!" Seeing us, she looked disappointed, then said, "You got the wrong house."

I had to hold her. "No, they said here!"

"Who said?"

"The children—"

Her mouth twitched. "Wish I'd heard them, I'd kick their butts. What'd you ask them?"

"We're hungry," Jim said.

"You just go somewhere else," she said briskly. "Both of you go. Those children were only teasing you. —What did they say?"

While I was wondering how to put it, Jim answered, "They said to go knock on the hoe's door."

"They did? Devils!" Suddenly she laughed. "It's a mystery to me how people not knowing anything about you will seven times out of ten come up with the truth. However, I am now what they call semi-retired. —You-all go about your business, you hear me?" She stepped back from the door to shut it.

"It's raining," I said quickly. It had just started; the wind blew a few drops on my neck.

She peered out again. "So it is. From the looks of you a little rain is not going to hurt you." Again she stepped back to close the door; again, paused. "What's that on your face, boy?"

Jim touched his cheek, finding the cut. The seam of the cut was black; around it was red.

The woman looked at me. "You been beating this boy? —Lord God, you've had some licks too!" she discovered. "Who did that to you all?"

"A man," Jim said.

"Your daddy do it?" We shook our heads no. "Say who?"

"Somebody we didn't know."

"Didn't *know?*" she cried, another look coming into her eyes. "Did he do anything besides hit you?"

My face must have told her.

"Son of a bitch! Low-down mother-fucker! Man do that would drink from a pisspot! Suck the snot from a dead man's nose! Eat fried dog shit! Lie down in pus and call maggots brother! —Come in this house and let me look at you."

We followed her.

The front room was furnished with a sofa and easy chairs, tables and a big radio. Everything looked new. There was a patterned rug on the floor. That much I saw as she led us through to a hallway that went to the kitchen, where the ceiling light was on and bright. She dropped into a rocking chair and pulled Jim to her. First she examined his face. Then she helped him take off his shirt and found dark marks on his back and shoulders.

"You got any clean clothes in that suitcase?" she asked me.

"Yes'm."

"Don't *yes'm* me. My name is Hazel Fay. Who're you and him?"

"Trudy Maynard."

"Jim Maynard."

"You both better take a bath. First him." She took Jim by the hand down the hall. I heard water running into the tub and pretty soon she came back into the kitchen. She had acted so fierce since we came into her house I was a little afraid of her. "Take off your dress and tell me what happened."

I did. The fact that she didn't seem surprised made it easy enough. All the time she was going over me with her eyes and hands, and now and then she'd grunt, more like talking to herself than to me. "You're not so bad," she said finally. "Nothing wrong that won't heal. A pussy can take a lot of punishment one way and another. How old are you?" I told her. "You ain't got much up there for going on fourteen, have you? Never mind, it'll come or it won't, and it makes no difference unless you plan to go into business. —When those children said what they did to you, did you understand what the word meant?"

"I think so."

"But he don't, does he?" I shook my head. "I was in a good House in New Orleans for over ten years. That's where I met Mr. Harris. He's a railroad engineer. Got a wife, two grown daughters. They all live down there. Me and him got friendly over the years, and he set me up here when I got tired of the game. Get Jim some drawers and go see if he's clean. Then you take a bath. I'll fix something to eat before you go on your way."

I found our suitcase by the front door where I'd left it and brought it inside. When I went to the bathroom, Jim had dried himself and was washing the sides of the tub the way I'd made him do at Uncle Earl's. I gave him clean underwear, a shirt, and a pair of wool knickers too big for him

Miss Verity had collected from her brother's congregation. When he was dressed, I told him to go to the kitchen while I took my bath.

Afterwards, I went back to the kitchen. Hazel Fay was frying ham and eggs, and Jim was setting plates and knives and forks on the table. What had struck me, though, opening the bathroom door, was Jim's voice rattling on at such a great rate I couldn't sort out what he was saying at the distance I was. He stopped talking just before I got to them, and Hazel Fay let loose a bellow of laughter. When I saw her, both her hands were helpless in the air as she staggered in a sort of stomping gait across the kitchen. Jim had commenced to laugh with her, a shrill, eager, little-boy's delight in her and himself. She saw me and leaned against the kitchen sink to gather strength. At last she was able to gulp out, "Jim been—he been—telling about—about the goldfish!"

Both gave themselves the pleasure of another round of laughter, and I found myself smiling like someone who hasn't heard all of a joke but wants to share in the fun. She dished up the ham and eggs and opened a loaf of light bread. "You ought to put him on the radio! Will Rogers is nothing at all compared to this boy. Eat."

We pulled chairs up to the big kitchen table and ate. She poured coffee into our cups and set the sugar bowl and cream pitcher where we could reach them easy. Then she poured coffee for herself, lit a cigarette, and sat down at the table. After watching us silently a few minutes she began to nod her head, as if to confirm something she had just told herself. "I believe you: you were hungry. I know *hungry* when I see it. It's years since I been hungry in the way of wanting and not having; but if you've known it, you don't forget it."

Not before or since have ham and eggs and bread and butter tasted so good to me. But as we ate—the ham and eggs gave out, and she encouraged us to continue with peanut butter and blackberry jam—I had a chance to study her.

She was the color of fried chicken. Her arms and body were well fleshed, but she was too supple in her movements to seem fat. Her hair was kinky black and morning-careless. Her teeth were whiter than milk, and I never in my life saw eyes like hers. They could love you, and they could laugh; they could kill you, or they could cry. Everything that "human" means was visible at some time in Hazel Fay's eyes and face. Years later I thought what an actress she might have made, only Negroes didn't get a chance in those days to do anything but sing and dance, and maybe Hazel Fay was too honest anyway to have made an actress. Whoever made up the phrase "whore with a heart of gold" must have hated whores, or goodness, and maybe both. Hazel Fay had been a whore, no questioning that. She talked about it to Jim and me as freely as somebody else might have said yes, they knew how to ride a bicycle and learned to make their own clothes from their mother. There was nothing the least dirty about anything she said or the way she said it, and I credit her with showing me and Jim the way to look at all kinds of life without getting into a fit and fever.

Finally we stopped eating and sat still. She looked from one to the other. "Are you satisfied?" she asked a little tauntingly. "Is your gut full, Jim?"

"Tight as a tick," Jim declared.

"You, Trudy?"

"I never ate so much."

She went to look out the window over the sink. "It's still

raining, so if y'all can stand up without the weight of your stomachs making you fall on your face, come let me show you my house. I'm proud of it, and nobody's seen it so I can brag about it but Mr. Harris."

First she told us a little more about Mr. Harris. He had left just before we knocked on her door. He'd be gone three days, she thought, doing his job for the railroad. He'd come and stay a day or two and then be gone a variable time, depending on his engine's schedule.

Mr. Harris had bought her the house five months ago, but it was in her name: Hazel Fay owned it. He'd had the bathroom built on; there had not been one before. There weren't many in the Day Street area. Most simply used pots until the contents were collected by what they called "the honey truck" because of the awful smell. Special water and power lines had to be run for Hazel's house, but Mr. Harris had seen to all of it, and the repairs, and the painting. He also stood good for the charge account she had at Weaver's Market.

"While I think of it, I better put in my order." We followed her through the hall to the living room, where the telephone was. She picked it up and gave the number to the exchange. "Mr. Weaver, this is Hazel Fay. You reckon this rain is going to continue? Sure looks like it, sure looks like it." She glanced at us. "Got your pencil ready? I want one pound of hot dogs." She paused deliberately after naming every item, and sometimes paused while she thought what else she might need. "Big can of Ritter pork and beans. Jar of mustard. Loaf of bread. Make that two loaves of bread. Two—no, three pounds spareribs; just crack them down the middle. Five pounds Irish potatoes. Two pounds sweet potatoes. Three pounds onions—don't send me no

rotten ones, because if you do, I'll send them right back."
She laughed. "Vinegar. Pound of coffee ground with an
ounce of chicory. Pound of butter. Two pounds compound
lard. Two packs Luckies. —Let me see. When the cakes
come in, pick me out something rich-looking, chocolate
with walnuts on top is good. Two quarts sweet milk, two
quarts buttermilk. I want a good big cabbage. Dozen
oranges." We waited through her longest pause. "No, I'm
just studying," she said into the receiver. "I reckon that'll
be all. If I think of anything else, I'll call you back. Oh—a
dozen eggs! I near forgot. No, Mr. Harris went to work this
morning. —Say what?" She laughed. "I got a couple of
children spending the day with me. Send me two Snickers,
two Mr. Goodbars, and a peanut brittle. Dozen oatmeal
cookies. Don't forget to send me the carbon of the order
with the prices; I'm keeping my eye on you, you know. Uh-
huh." With another laugh she said, "Good-by," and hung
up.

Turning to us she said, "You like my rug here? Nine by
twelve. What they call Oriental. How you like *that*? That's
my radio, that big whale in the corner, plays good but
scares me to death sometimes with the static, enough to
make a corpse sit up and whistle 'Dixie.' Living room suite
come all together, two chairs and sofa, and when the man
found out I was paying cash instead of a dollar down and a
dollar a week the rest of my life, he threw in that table and
two floor lamps."

From the living room she took us into the bedroom.
There was a double bed, not yet made up, a chest of drawers, a big wardrobe, and what she called her "vanity" table
and bench. On the chest was a set of men's hairbrushes
with silver backs and a tie clip and matching cuff links.

Across the hall from the bedroom was a room that hadn't been furnished. She opened the door to let us look in. "Don't go getting any ideas," she said. "This is going to be my sewing room. Always wanted a room just for sewing. I love to sew. That's my new Singer at the window to catch the daylight. I hate to use the electric light while I'm sewing unless I have to. Makes my eyes hurt. First time I had my own machine. I used to sew clothes for half the girls in the House down in New Orleans, white, colored, one Mexican, and a midget called herself Mary Pickford. All women have about the same interest in clothes. If you were going to stay awhile I'd make you something, Trudy, that don't look like a flour sack, but it just ain't going to rain that long. I'm getting me a big table so I can cut my patterns on it without breaking my back bending over the bed, and I been thinking maybe I'd get me"—she turned to Jim and gave him a slap on his behind—"some goldfish to keep me company. Don't want a cat. Piece of cloth ain't safe with a cat in the house. They'll pull threads with their claws or sleep on it and leave a million hairs." She closed the door as we left. "Don't like a door open on an unfurnished room. Looks like a waiting grave."

The rain was our friend that day. The groceries were delivered by a Negro boy about sixteen named Ed. He wore an old cracked raincoat, but he was sopping wet anyway. He looked at us while Hazel checked over her groceries and then made him a bologna sandwich, but she didn't offer to say who we were and we didn't volunteer. About twelve o'clock, when Hazel heated the pork and beans and boiled the hot dogs, she brewed a big brown pot of tea. "Always want tea when it rains; soothes me. We used to have it at the House. Bunch of whores sitting around in their kimonos drinking tea like ladies at a bridge party! You reckon that rain will never stop?"

It did, a little before three o'clock.

By that time Hazel had talked a lot, and Jim had talked a lot, and so had I. None of us tried to "tell" things, but just in talking we told enough so that Hazel stopped being a stranger to us, and she was no longer saying, "When the rain stops, you're to go." One of the things I'd learned about her was that she was lonesome. I don't think she missed the old life, but she did miss company.

"Ignorant niggers around here won't even say how-de-do. Half of them ain't married to the man they live with, but they treat me funny because Mr. Harris is a white man. How you like that? God knows what they'll think when they see you spending the day here!" She frowned and was silent a little while. "Tell you what—let's go walking and show them—not that they don't already know from Ed! I spect you-all better stay and help me eat those spareribs for supper; don't know what made me order so many. And if you don't mind a pallet on the floor for one night, you're welcome to it. Better than sleeping back of some billboard on wet ground. Tomorrow after breakfast, if the weather clears, you can go on your way."

The sun had come out, but by the time Hazel changed her shoes and put on her coat, it was clouding again. Just as we turned into Day Street, we heard the school bell ring, and children began to run out of the school building. "Let's have some fun," Hazel said. "Trudy, you nudge me when you see her."

We stood and waited, and pretty soon the big girl of that morning came along with her friends. Oh, how she gaped—oh, how she glared! Life gives few small rewards to compare with paying off past rudeness. The big revenges may leave a sour taste, but the little ones are sweet. Yet even as I enjoyed her surprise, knowing she had meant us mischief that morning, I owned that I had her to thank for sending us to Hazel Fay.

CHAPTER 14

I woke on the pallet in the living room knowing right away where I was. Jim wasn't there. After washing face and hands I dressed and went to find him. He and Hazel were just coming into the kitchen from the back yard, scraping their shoes on the steps. Hazel said, "Let's have some battercakes," and stirred the bowl of batter she'd mixed and left standing. "I had coffee but waited to eat with you. Jim, get y'all a glass of milk so you won't starve." Jim and I drank milk and set the table while Hazel fried ham and cooked the battercakes. "I was showing Jim my yard. I been setting out bulbs for next spring, and you know something? The neighbors on both sides came separately to the fence to find out who you are. Never said a word to me before, just tossed their ugly heads and looked away when they saw me. Now I'm respectable. I told the first one you were my cousins from the country. She laughed and said, 'You keeping them chirrun for your Mr. Harris?' —See? They know his name like they know everything else. Of course, they have to assume I'm working for white folks to make it all right. Dumb heifers."

In the yard Jim had talked some more about Aunt Olive, and they both had obviously enjoyed their conversation. "Women can be harder than men," Hazel mused. "Meaner too, excluding an occasional born son of a bitch like the one harmed you. This aunt sounds like Mr. Harris's wife Eunice, although he's too much a gentleman to complain about her to me. However, from what I gather she can't cook and is too lazy to hump. They always have names like Eunice and Olive. Now, Mary—there's a good name. I never knew a 'Mary' I couldn't get along with."

We were at the table. I was eating. Hazel was eating and talking. Jim was eating and giggling. "Jim," Hazel said after a pause to swallow, "what are you carrying on about?"

"The way you talk."

"It won't hurt you to hear me and you may learn something," she said. "I been studying about you two while you were sleeping half the good day through."

I said guiltily, "We always woke early down home, but last night was the first good sleep we've had since leaving Miss Verity." We had talked about Miss Verity to her yesterday.

"If you say she's all right, I take your word for it, but me, I am suspicious of Christian women. What I been studying about and come up with is this: Mr. Harris won't be back till Friday morning. Unless you got big plans you haven't let me in on, you can stay here and eat good and rest up and leave early Friday before he gets here. He won't come till ten or eleven o'clock. I have never seen him in his working clothes. He washes and changes at the station. He's particular, Mr. Harris. Keeps his fingernails perfect. Sometimes even lets me put clear polish on them. It's kind of a play-game with him; I tease him into it. However, Mr. Harris is a real man-man; some might call him stern and exacting. That is why you oughtn't to be here when he comes. I like him to know he'll find peace and comfort. Mr. Harris appreciates a woman; many do not. —I assume you don't mind staying on a little?" Jim shook his head left and right, I shook mine up and down, both of us meaning the same thing. "You can help me do some things I haven't been able to do by myself. There's a big place called Oak Park that's got wild animals, they say, and I want to see them. You know what a park is?"

I said I did; Jim said he didn't. Hazel explained to him.

"Why couldn't you go by yourself?" Jim asked.

"They don't allow colored," she said, "unless—here's where you come in. They don't allow colored unless they bring white children, like a nursemaid, you know."

Hazel pushed her plate away, wiped a drip from the lip of the syrup pitcher and sucked her finger. Then she pulled her coffee nearer and lit a cigarette. "Let's clean house in a hurry and make ourselves a picnic lunch and go to Oak Park and see the wild animals!"

We all pitched into the housework and then took the Cloverdale bus Downtown, where we transferred to one that took us to Oak Park. Going through town we passed the Paramount Theater. A show called *Horse Feathers* was playing, and Jim asked me if Edward G. Robinson was in it and I told him not that I could see. That got us talking about the one picture show we'd been to. Hazel said she couldn't go to the white theaters and didn't often go to the colored one because it didn't get very good things. Its name was the Pekin. Jim told her the whole story of *The Hatchet Man.*

Oak Park was a big place, and we walked into it like we owned it. The wild animals turned out to be deer and monkeys, and a few mosquitoes left over from summer and revived by yesterday's rain. The deer were tame enough to come close but wouldn't let us touch them through the wire fence. Hazel made us stand well back from the monkeys, although we all looked at them a long time, in fact, until Hazel said, "Let's go spread our picnic. They look too much like us, make me nervous."

Hazel had made good sandwiches, deviled ham with cucumber relish, sliced pineapple with mayonnaise, and peanut butter and jelly. We finished off with oranges and oatmeal cookies and went back to look at the monkeys. Jim said they were almost as good as a picture show. Hazel looked at him intently for a minute, then said, "Come on, I'll take you to a real picture show, the one playing at the Paramount you nearly broke your neck turning around on the bus to look at. Only I can't go with you."

"Let's not go," I said.

Unwilling to give up a show so easily, Jim said, "What's playing at the Pekin? Would they let us in?"

"Don't ever turn down a chance to go to the Paramount, Jim. They say it's the best picture show in Montgomery. Besides, I got an idea worth trying."

We got off the bus at Court Square without bothering to transfer because the Paramount Theater was close enough to walk from there. In front of Montgomery Fair Hazel gave me a dime. "Go to Kress and buy a sack of those chocolate-covered peanuts Jim's been talking about. Then come back here and wait for me."

She went into the store, and we did what she said. I wouldn't let us eat any candy until she showed up. When she did, lo and behold, she was carrying a package under her arm that turned out to be her dress, and she was wearing a white uniform. As we gaped at her, she turned around, showing off. "How you like it? What you see before you is me in a nursemaid uniform. My only fear is that I now look more high-class than you-all." She held out her hand. "Give me nourishment while I think." I shook candy into her hand.

When we got to the Paramount, Hazel told us to stand in sight but not too close. "Trudy," she said, "I want you to put on a mean face. Think of that man beat y'all up and what you'd like to do to him some day. Jim, if I turn around and point at you, you jump up and down, not a whole lot, just a time or two. Understand?" We nodded, and she went to buy our tickets. She had what appeared to be an earnest conversation with the ticket seller, who kept shaking her head at first. Then Hazel turned and pointed at us. I looked mean, and Jim jumped up and down. The ticket seller stared, then pushed something that released two tickets, as Hazel gave her some money. I wondered if Hazel was not going with us after all. However, she came over and made a show of herding us inside the theater, to act like a nursemaid, I supposed.

Well, I thought we'd all die laughing. We ran out of candy, and I went to the lobby and bought popcorn with money Hazel slipped me. Jim said he'd never seen anybody as pretty as Thelma Todd, not even Mama. There was a newsreel too, mostly about Franklin D. Roosevelt trying to get elected President.

Afterwards, we caught the Day Street bus on the other side of Montgomery Street and went home. Sitting by Hazel I asked her who she was voting for, and she said nobody but she liked the look of Franklin D. Roosevelt better than Herbert Hoover, who always looked like he'd eaten too much and it hadn't agreed with him. Anyway, she added, everybody said prosperity was just around the corner. Herself, she liked a glass of beer, and it would be nice to buy it instead of having to make her own home brew. It was getting dark and lights were coming on in the houses on Day Street. Most of them were kerosene flickers that had a cosy look but turned eerie when somebody carried a lamp from one room to another.

As we got off the bus by the schoolhouse, I asked Hazel why she'd bought only two tickets for the picture show. "One for you and one for Jim," she explained. "I didn't count because I was the nursemaid and not supposed to enjoy myself. Being colored saves money now and then."

"What were you and her talking about so long before she'd sell you the tickets?"

"She didn't want me to go in, but leave you and come back for you when the show was over. I told her I couldn't do that because you had a habit of running away from home and your Mama had told me never to leave your side."

"Why did you want Jim to jump up and down?"

"Jim was my trump. I told her he had fits and one of us must sit on either side of him."

CHAPTER 15

Thursday morning Hazel made me a dress out of one of hers. It started by her giving me funny looks as we ate breakfast. When we were done and just sitting there talking, she lit her second cigarette before saying, "I don't claim I can make you into another Clara Bow, but I can get you looking less like Moon Mullins. You are nearly fourteen, and it is time you begun to take on the appearance of a girl. To start with I got a red crepe de Chine dress I never cared for because I could never get it to fit. It was always too fat or too skinny for me. Some dresses are like that. If you got no objections, I'll start ripping and sewing. Jim, how about you wash the dishes for me?"

By ten o'clock the dress was re-made and mine. I never saw hands work so fast and with so much skill as Hazel's did with that cloth and sewing machine. I didn't believe it was me when I stood in front of her big wardrobe mirror, and Jim, sidling in the doorway, said, "You sure don't look like yourself."

"This is the new, true Trudy Maynard," Hazel said. "Breaks men's hearts and snaps her fingers at their piteous wails. You ever thought of singing with a band?"

"I can't sing," I said.

"She sure can't," Jim added.

"All right," I said, looking at him in the mirror. "I'm warning you."

"Well, you can't," he said. "You sound like a goat." He imitated a goat.

"Doesn't stop some of them," Hazel said. "Of course, the shoes don't go with it." We all looked down at my old Buster Browns. "Black, high-heel pumps," she said, "and we ought to do something else with your hair."

"Get her a whole new head," Jim said.

Hazel threw a hairbrush at him, and he ran out giggling. Hazel pulled and twisted my hair this way and that, both of us standing in front of the mirror, her behind me. "Every way looks worse than the one before," she decided. "But no woman was born with hair that suited her. Takes a lot of thought and experiment. I'll study on it. Meantime, you let your hair grow and stop cutting it with a meat cleaver. Then wash it with something to make it softer. What you been using, Borax?"

I changed back into my old dress and folded the red crepe de Chine in tissue paper Hazel gave me, handling it as carefully as angel food cake. I'd never had anything so pretty, and it was from then I stopped thinking of myself as ugly. I knew I was plain and would always be, but Hazel had given me hope that I wasn't hopeless.

I helped Hazel clear up the scraps from the floor of her sewing room and then she took me and Jim with her on a shopping trip to Weaver's Market. Mr. Weaver had known somebody was staying with Hazel, and I reckoned she had decided to show him who was. I was interested to see the way he behaved to her, friendly but not familiar. It was clear he considered her a good customer and gave her the best he had. Mr. Weaver offered to set us up to cold drinks, and we accepted. I didn't see the clerk that had called me "young lady" on Sunday, and when I asked where he was, found out it was Mr. Weaver's own boy Wade, and he was in school, being in the eleventh grade, and worked only weekends and the afternoons he didn't have band practice. He played the trumpet. Hazel decided on sausage for our midday dinner and a three-pound cut of beef chuck to cook in gravy for supper. There was a sizable heap of groceries by the time she'd looked and picked and asked for anything she wanted and didn't see. Mr. Weaver offered to deliver, but Hazel said we'd save Ed a trip on his bicycle and do the toting ourselves. Each of us carried a big sack, and Jim was sagging pretty low by the time we got to the front door.

It's hard to say who was more surprised when we went in, us or Mr. Harris, for Mr. Harris was sitting there in the living room reading the Montgomery *Advertiser*. He was a thin, not to say skinny, man with gray hair combed neat over his head. He wore rimless eyeglasses, and he looked dignified in his gray suit as he got up and put the newspaper aside.

"Well!—Well, I'll be dogged!" Hazel said in surprise, but happy to see him too. "You, Trudy and Jim, take this stuff on to the kitchen; I'll be there in a minute or two."

I took her sack of groceries from her, and we left them. As we unpacked, the talk from the living room was mostly Hazel. She still sounded surprised but glad he was there, and not the least bit put out, or caught out. Mr. Harris's voice was lower than hers, and we couldn't understand what he was saying. I remembered that we were supposed to have been gone when he got there. He'd come earlier than he'd said, but the house was his, or Hazel's through him.

Pretty soon Hazel came into the kitchen, her eyes bright. "Here's a dollar," she said, handing me a bill. "I want y'all to get the bus Downtown and have yourself something to eat at the counter at Kress—I understand they have a pretty good special for a quarter—and go to a picture show, the Strand or Tivoli since you've seen the Paramount. When you get out, but not before four or five o'clock—and not too much after, you hear?—come on home. I need a little time to tell Mr. Harris about you. Now, Trudy"— she shook me by the arm—"don't get any of your running-away ideas. Do like I say. Late in the afternoon, come home."

I had no hope of Mr. Harris. Hazel had indicated that he was a hard man, and he certainly looked it. However, when Jim and I got on the bus, I told him we'd do what she said. We got off at Court Square and studied the pictures outside the Strand. One hand-lettered sign said: "Montgomery's Own Tallulah Bankhead." The name of the picture was *Thunder Below*, and Charles Bickford was in it too. Then we went on to Kress and had a good look around. That store—in fact, any five-and-ten-cent store— was Wonderland to us, perhaps because we were from the country. It didn't matter that we couldn't use, didn't need and wouldn't even want most of the things. I think it was their abundance and variety, as well as the colors and smells that held us spellbound. I didn't buy any candy, though we looked at it. Staying even that little time with Hazel had made us take food for granted.

However, I reminded myself that we'd soon be leaving Hazel's house. I steered Jim firmly past the counter that held the red pencil box he had wanted that other time we were there; even so he gave it a look. The eating counter at the back was crowded; there wasn't a single empty seat. Everything looked so shiny and bustling, and everybody looked so sure of themselves and so much better dressed than we did, I felt shy about waiting. Jim had begun to look timid too, so without saying we would, we wandered back through the big store and on to the sidewalk.

Across the street was a Woolworth five-and-ten we'd never been to; we picked our way over and went in. It was a little dark and shabby compared to Kress. I looked to see what their eating counter was like. It wasn't as daunting as the one at Kress, so I found two empty seats together and we were all but climbing into them when I saw Aunt Olive not six feet away. She hadn't seen us; she was studying spools of thread on a rack. Grabbing Jim by the hand, I got us out as fast as I could, short of running, and didn't explain until we were half a block away. When he heard Aunt Olive's name, he was for sure-enough running.

Dexter Avenue was full of people; many looked like they worked Downtown and were on their lunch hour. I decided the best thing to do was to cut to the back streets. The next over running parallel to Dexter was Monroe, and it looked poorer than Dexter. We went over one more to Madison before I felt safe and wandered along until we saw a diner that had some empty stools and went in to look at their prices. There was a special plate for twenty cents consisting of pork chops and rice and gravy and cream corn. By then we were hungry enough so it sounded all right, and besides it was a nickel cheaper than the Kress plate Hazel had suggested.

We ordered and ate and didn't talk. We felt better then, less scared of having seen Aunt Olive. A meal always makes me feel better. When we left the diner, I asked Jim if he wanted to go to the Strand. He said, "What if Aunt Olive is there?"

"It doesn't look to me like a picture she'd go to, if she ever goes to any," I said. "But if it's true about the rats she sure won't be at the Tivoli, nor will Lucien and old Alice after school."

From newspaper ads I knew where all the picture shows were, and we found the Tivoli on Commerce Street easily. The show was George O'Brien in *Riders of the Purple Sage*, and there weren't any rats. That was our first Western. We saw it twice, and Jim and I thought of George O'Brien as one of our heroes for some years after that. We'd never had heroes before we started going to picture shows. People had talked a lot about Lindy and Jack Dempsey, but as far as I was concerned, they were peewees compared to George O'Brien. Much as we enjoyed the picture, I couldn't forget what was ahead of us, and I wondered where we'd end up sleeping tonight.

That made me feel low, and Jim could see I did when we got out on the sidewalk after the show. As we poked our way along Commerce Street to Court Square to wait for the Day Street bus, I added up in my head what we'd spent: forty cents at the diner on Madison, twenty cents for George O'Brien, a dime for the bus to town. We'd need another dime for the bus back to Hazel's. That left twenty cents. I ought by rights to give it back to her. Well, I would, I decided, I certainly would. She'd been good to us.

Then I happened to glance at Jim. I had never wasted sympathy on him, but I suddenly felt sorry for him. The look in his eyes was so dreading. I found myself saying, "Before we go back, we're going to Kress and buy you that pencil box." Night turned to day on his face. He started to run, and I ran after him. I didn't catch up with him until he'd got there and had the box in his hands looking it over. It was only painted cardboard, but the snap sounded good when he opened and closed it. There were two long pencils, a pen staff and two points, a six-inch ruler and an eraser, the smooth end for pencil and the darker, rougher end for ink. I gave the clerk a dime and we went out to stand in front of Klein's jewelry store to wait for our bus.

Jim said, after fingering the box awhile, "Can I open it?"

I said, "Go ahead. You own it."

CHAPTER 16

Thinking about it in later years I marveled that George Harris and Hazel Fay ever got together. In the first place, I wondered how Mr. Harris had found himself in a whorehouse. The answer, I suppose, is that need and desperation can make stranger bedfellows than love and war. And I have only to remind myself of how different all of us are from the way we look.

Mr. Harris was, no doubt, stern and exacting in many of his dealings with other people—and certainly with himself—but to Hazel he had given whatever trust and innocence he had left. To say she loved him for it is to say only the truth. How different might it have been for them if they had come together forty or fifty years later, when the South had sorted out its past and begun to live beyond the old hatreds and sour accommodations. There have been things to touch my heart in the changes that have come, but none, I think, more than a couple I saw recently on a street in Atlanta: a white man and a Negro woman, both of them sixty-five or seventy years old. They were ordinary in clothes and features. But something in the way they walked together, not talking to each other—indeed, the very naturalness of their silence indicated to me that they were a couple who had lived long together, and that only now, after all the years they had shared, did they dare do something as simple as walk along the street together like any ordinary couple. When I see the occasional young mixed pair these days, for all their studied nonchalance so very conscious of their daring, I think: you don't know what bravery is.

I can't say why Jim and I were not shocked at the friendship of Hazel and George Harris. Perhaps because we needed them, although I prefer to think it was because we loved Hazel. Living as we had, isolated in a small town and later on a farm, we'd had little contact with Negroes. Southern children were not taught or even told how things were between the races; they were supposed to be born knowing.

When we got to Hazel's that night, I thought it best to knock on the door, but as nobody answered, Jim and I went in. Finding no one in the front of the house, we went back to the kitchen, where we could see a light and hear Hazel's voice. I called her name and we went in. She had a cooking fork in one hand. With the other she was patting

Mr. Harris on the cheek. He sat in her rocking chair in shirt sleeves with a blue garter on the left one, his tie neatly tied.

"So you-all are home!" Hazel said cheerily.

"We came for the suitcase," I said.

"Uh-huh." She winked at Mr. Harris, who suddenly looked as shy as I felt at having come upon them the way we had. But he smiled, trying to be friendly about it. "Uh-huh. Where you going to next?"

Jim and I looked at each other. "Down the road a piece," Jim said airily.

Hazel nodded. "Well, night's no time to start. You think so, Mr. Harris?"

He shook his head. "No. I wouldn't say so."

"Of course, if you're bound and determined." Hazel shrugged and lifted the lid on a deep skillet on the stove. "Don't know what I'll do with all this chuck beef and onions and potatoes. Added some hot peppers and tomatoes like they do in New Orleans. Sure like to have you stay and help eat it, but I reckon you know best."

"We'll stay!" Jim said.

I hold the memory of that room and night close before letting it go. At last we were welcome somewhere; we *felt* welcome. Mr. Harris never dropped his reserve with us, and perhaps never had with anyone except Hazel. But without losing his shyness, which actually had the effect of making me feel easier, he relaxed and enjoyed himself. His face pink with pleasure and the warmth of the stove, he seemed to have just discovered the satisfaction of sitting in a kitchen while a meal was prepared by loving hands.

I helped Hazel with supper, and Jim set the table. While he was doing that, Hazel had him tell Mr. Harris about the goldfish, and he liked it nearly as much as she did the first time she heard it. The nervousness Jim felt before coming back to the house vanished. He showed them the red pencil box. Hazel exclaimed over it fulsomely. One of her qualities was the ability to see the worth of a thing in someone else's eyes, no matter how little it might mean to her. Mr. Harris examined the box thoughtfully and asked Jim if he'd gone to school. Jim told him no-sir, but that Mama had taught him, and Mr. Harris went off to the bedroom and came back a minute later with a thick tablet of paper and said, "Here. You can practice on this."

Jim was Mr. Harris's friend from then on. In his pride of ownership it had not occurred to him, as it had not to me, that he had nothing to use his new tools on. Mr. Harris found him a bottle of ink after supper and showed him how to set a pen point in the cork end of the staff and hold the point in a match flame until it would take ink.

And now and then Mr. Harris made a little joke with Jim, not meant to be funny, just friendly. At one point he asked him how he intended to vote in the election, Democrat or Republican.

"Franklin D. Roosevelt!" Jim sang out, and all of us laughed.

I insisted we wash the dishes after we'd all eaten the chocolate pie Hazel had made and cooled that afternoon while we were gone. When we were done in the kitchen, Hazel called us into the living room to sit with her and Mr. Harris. They were listening to the radio. Jim staked himself to a piece of the floor under a lamp where he worked with pencils and paper the rest of the evening. Even the radio, which was still a novelty to both of us, couldn't supplant his new possession. When Hazel saw he was sleepy, she told us to roll out our pallet on the floor of her sewing room. We did, and went to sleep with the low sound of radio music coming through the wall.

Nothing had been said about our staying beyond that night, but I think we understood that we would. During the evening Hazel had made a remark about going to town tomorrow or the next day to look over cotton goods for material to make me some everyday dresses. And as we'd left them for bed, Mr. Harris had told Jim he'd give him half a dollar if Roosevelt was elected President, although he must have known he almost certainly would be.

The next morning Mr. Harris went off by himself for an hour and came back in a truck with a man who proceeded to unload and at Hazel's direction set up two single beds in the sewing room. I was so overcome I said, "I don't mind the floor or sleeping with Jim."

Hazel said, "Maybe Jim minds. A boy likes to be by himself now and then; ain't that right, Jim?"

He smirked at her in such a superior way I wanted to kick his butt.

CHAPTER 17

Two weeks later Mr. Roosevelt had been elected President and everybody was talking about beer and better times. Jim had won and collected his fifty-cent piece from Mr. Harris and bought two secondhand books he couldn't read at a place on Perry Street called the Booklovers Shop. He was, however, learning to read; he had started to school at the one on Sayre Street and Mildred Street.

Here's how it happened.

True to her word, Hazel bought some dress material on that first Saturday as soon as Mr. Harris left us and worked all day Sunday at her sewing machine. Monday morning she'd finished four what she called everyday dresses for me, although each was out of different material and done a little differently with ribbons, or buttons, or fancy collars and cuffs. I began to feel as dressy as Alice.

Monday afternoon we went to Oak Park again, and Monday evening Hazel kept studying Jim, who spent most of his time when he was in the house with his pencil box and tablet. He drew pictures that were really just diagrams of trees and houses and people, the usual things children try to draw, but his were all tiny to get the most he could out of his supply of paper. He also printed the words Mama had taught him to write such as BOY, CAT, DOG, JIM, RUN.

When Mr. Harris wasn't there, the three of us would go to the living room after supper to hear whatever was on the radio. We didn't have favorite programs yet; we just listened to what came out. But Monday night Hazel didn't pay it much attention for a while, studying Jim as she was, like something about him bothered her. Suddenly, right in the middle of some woman singing "It's Only a Shanty in Old Shanty Town" she said to me, "Now I got you on the road to fame and fortune I better see to him. I have decided what to do at last." I asked her what but she said, "Ask me no questions, I'll tell you no lies."

Jim kept on drawing like it didn't concern him, and Hazel then relaxed and listened to the radio.

Next morning, while Jim and I washed the breakfast dishes, I could hear her talking on the telephone. Pretty soon she came back to the kitchen. "See you about done. Looks nice," she said automatically, as she always did when she praised us for something we'd done for her or the house. "Trudy, I'm going somewhere, and I want you to put on one of your new frocks and come with me. Jim, you reckon you can keep yourself company while we're gone?"

We walked. Hazel said it wasn't far and she wanted to stretch her legs and get her mind rolling. Not until we left the house did she tell me we were going to see Mrs. Weaver. She had telephoned Mr. Weaver at the store and told him what she wanted to do and he suggested she go talk to his wife. She'd agreed and he had telephoned Mrs. Weaver we were coming. The Weavers lived on Mildred Street east of Mobile Street in a big old ugly two-story house with rocking chairs and a rusting glider on the front porch. Hazel led us down the driveway to the back yard, where we found Mrs. Weaver hanging clothes on a line.

I had expected her to be fat for no better reason than that her husband sold meat and groceries, but Mrs. Weaver surprised me by being an uncommonly thin woman. There was nothing puny about her though, as we could see by the easy way she lifted the big basket of wrung-out wet wash and moved it along under the clothesline. She had clothespins in her mouth, and she continued to work until we went up close.

"You're Mrs. Weaver?" Hazel asked her.

She nodded.

"Mr. Weaver told you we'd come?"

She nodded again and took two remaining clothespins from between her teeth, dropping them into a large dress pocket with others.

"You know who we are?" Hazel continued.

By then the woman had looked both of us over. "Yes," she said to Hazel, "I know who you are." Her voice was level, pitched in the middle, neither high nor low. It told me nothing about her and nothing of what she thought of us. Her eyes came to me. "So you're the girl."

133

"Yes, ma'am. Gertrude Maynard is my name."

"My husband told me why you were coming. Sit down on the steps over there till I finish what I'm doing, and I'll talk to you."

"Can we help you?" I asked.

She shook her head. "I do my own work." She added formally after a moment, "I thank you," as if grudging the courtesy but determined to be fair.

Hazel and I sat on the bottom step without talking while she hung up the rest of her washing. It was mostly men's shirts and drawers and handkerchiefs, which she tied to the line with small knots to save clothespins. The yard smelled of soap and wet cloth as the wind blew toward the steps where we sat. Finished, Mrs. Weaver carried her empty basket with one hand and with the other picked up an old kitchen chair she'd sawed the back off to make a work stool for the back yard.

When she'd sat down near us but not so close as to suggest friendliness, she said to me, "How old is your brother?"

"Jim's seven."

"Why hasn't he been to school? You-all been tramping around?" Those were her first words indicating a judgment.

I told her briefly about us, about Mama's dying and Papa's leaving, about our coming to Montgomery and Uncle Earl's planning to put us in the Orphans' Home. I kept to facts, and the way I told them was as dry as she talked. She frowned, but only in a listening way.

When I finished, she said to Hazel, "You intend to keep them with you?"

"For the time being," Hazel said.

"What about you?" Mrs. Weaver said to me. "You wanting to go to school too?"

"No, ma'am," I said firmly. "My school days are over."

"How old are you?" she said.

"Old enough not to go to school."

Her eyes took on a look of warning; then she must have understood I hadn't meant to be pert, only cautious. "Well," she said, and left the word hanging without further encouragement.

"I want to find work," I said.

"There's no work even for those who know how to do useful things, and you don't, I bet."

I said, "I can cook and clean house. I took care of ours when Mama was sick." I saw she was unimpressed, so I added, "I worked in a store one time." That was very near but not quite a lie. Hazel looked at me surprised until she seemed to remember my telling her about the fat man and the molded bread and oil sausage.

"That's a fact," Hazel said.

"It's none of my business," Mrs. Weaver said briskly, implying that neither did it interest her. "My own son went to Sayre Street Grammar School when he was little. He finishes Lanier, that's the senior high, a year from next June."

"He plays trumpet in the band," I said.

It was her turn to be surprised. She nodded. She was one for nodding, as if every word saved was a dollar in the bank. "Sayre Street School isn't far, a few blocks, but when your brother is enrolled, they'll ask questions like his parents' name and what they do and where they live. They'll find out who you live with." She looked at Hazel. "They won't accept you as his guardian."

"I thought of that," Hazel said. "And I thought what I'd do when I take him to be enrolled: I'd wear my white nursemaid uniform and say his mama was an invalid and his daddy was a traveling man and I was the one hired to look after him."

"What would you give as their address?" Hazel didn't answer. "If you give them yours, they'll know it's the colored section. No white folks live out there. Everybody knows that."

"Still," Hazel said stubbornly, "it ain't against the law for white folks to live there, is it?"

"They might come to check," Mrs. Weaver said in a way that suggested what they'd think if they did.

We were all silent for a minute or two. On the way Hazel had told me to let her do most of the talking; she wanted me with her mainly for my presence.

"I don't see any way out of it," Mrs. Weaver said.

Hazel had been frowning to herself while we were quiet and now she spoke. "There's a way," she said. "There's a way I've thought of. I take Jim to enroll and say what I said I'd say about his mama and daddy, but when they ask where they-all live, give them your and Mr. Weaver's address here on Mildred Street."

Mrs. Weaver looked at her in astonishment. "You're not timid, are you?" she said in her dry way.

"No'm," Hazel said. And went on quickly, "You own this whole house, don't you, Mrs. Weaver?"

She nodded.

"You and your family live downstairs and rent out two apartments upstairs?"

She nodded, her eyes showing no surprise that Hazel knew this.

"Well, if anybody from the school comes out to see about him, you could tell them they live upstairs but got no phone and his mama is sick and can't see nobody."

Mrs. Weaver stared at her. "You're asking me to tell a lie."

Hazel said, "Yes'm. But only if necessary. Only if they come poking around."

"Why in the name of heaven do you suppose I'd do such a thing for you?" She'd decided time had come to drop manners.

"It's for the child, not me."

"A child I don't know, haven't even seen. No." She stood. "I'm sorry. I don't lie. I don't think this is a good idea. I don't think it's a good idea at all. When Mr. Weaver told me white children were staying there with you, I didn't think *that* was a good idea either."

Hazel said, "You think they'd be better off in a Home?"

"Maybe they would. That's what their uncle thought, and I don't hold with going against kin."

"No, ma'am," I said, "we wouldn't. I've told Jim, no matter what, we're not going into any Home."

"None of this concerns me," Mrs. Weaver said. "I'm sorry, but I'm busy this morning and you may as well go." She picked up her basket to go into the house, but Hazel did not get up to let her by and I stuck to my seat beside her.

"Mrs. Weaver," Hazel said, "I hate to say this, but you force me. These are hard times. I'm a good cash customer at Mr. Weaver's store. I expect every account he's got is important to him. I know for a fact that most of the people running bills with him haven't been paid up for years. Every payday they go in and pay what they can and he goes on giving them credit, because if he didn't he might lose his chance of ever collecting on their back bills, and they'd take what cash they had and go trade somewhere else. Meantime he's got a lot of debt money riding on his books, and every *cash* account is that much more important. Do I make myself clear?"

"Not yet." Mrs. Weaver's eyes didn't blink.

"I could take my business somewhere else."

Mrs. Weaver didn't change expression, but her words snapped like a whip. "Get up and go!"

We got up and started down the driveway. We were almost at the sidewalk when she called, "Wait a minute." Still carrying the empty clothes basket she came halfway to meet us and said, "I'll think about it, but I don't promise a thing."

CHAPTER 18

The first grade classroom was full that year. Because of his age they decided to let Jim try the second grade, and he made it. He was so glad to be there and so willing about everything, I think his teacher, Miss Kramer, gave him extra help and pushed him. He must have stuck out because he was new and because he looked and talked so countrified, but also because he liked school, whereas most of the others were just waiting for recess so they could go outdoors and play. Jim worshiped Miss Kramer. Everything she said to him was Truth Revealed. It was Miss Kramer this and Miss Kramer that, until I'd have hated the sound of her name if we hadn't been beholden to her for the trouble she took with him. Almost all the papers he did at school and brought home had a little gold star pasted on, whether it was a drawing or writing, and she saw to it he got his books free. She must have seen he was poor, in spite of Hazel's wearing her white uniform to enroll him, but to save his pride told him it wasn't necessary for him to buy books with the semester so far along.

Mr. Harris came and went. He was friendly to us and didn't appear to mind our being there. Whatever Hazel liked was all right with him. When he was there, I kept me and Jim out of the house except mealtimes and at night. Of course, Jim was at school in the morning and early afternoon, so I took to walking about the Day Street area by myself. I didn't think of it as poor, though it was. It has always been my favorite part of Montgomery, mainly because it was where we got our first toehold, but also because I liked it for itself. It had the look of having grown naturally, not of having been laid out in a square pattern the way most sections of the city were. Yards were seldom fenced, and people drifted about freely. The side streets were like lanes. There was only one big street, Day Street, and that's where everything important was: the school, the stores, the biggest church.

I wandered about and got to know people, and they began to know me. A lot of women who didn't work away from home as cooks or maids took in washing; in those days few people had their own washing machines. The air was usually full of the smells of soap and starch, of clothes drying on lines outdoors, of the smoke of outdoor fires around the washpots made of scraps of wood and anything else that came handy like orange and apple crates. From indoors drifted the good clean smell of ironing done with those old-fashioned heavy black irons that were heated on a stove or in a fireplace, and whose flat bottoms were the smoothest thing I have ever run my hand over.

I also went to Mr. Weaver's store with Hazel, and, when Mr. Harris was there, for her. They never left the house together. I came to know all at the store—Mr. Weaver, of course, who was his own butcher; Wade, who came in some afternoons and all day Saturday and Sunday morning until one o'clock, when the store closed. Ed was the delivery boy, thin and always seeming to breathe heavy because of the bicycle riding he did. It was an old beat-up bicycle that took a lot of muscle and wind to pedal. The other clerk was named Harvey Miller. He was a rangy man somewhere in his thirties, and he laughed a whole lot, but I decided I didn't like him. I didn't like the way he treated people who came in the store. His manner looked friendly but was only familiar. He teased the children. If a man was young, it was, "What'll you have, boy?" If he was old, he called him "uncle." He addressed females as "girl" or "auntie" depending on their age. He also thought it was fun to put dry peas in a blown-up paper bag so they'd rattle, and tie the bag to the tail of any stray dog he caught or coaxed into the store, hollering loud to scare the dog before he turned him loose. Naturally the dog would scoot away fast, out of his mind with fear, and Harvey Miller would lean in the door laughing till he had to wipe the tears from his eyes.

Business came in spurts. There were always people waiting at the door at six o'clock in the morning when the store opened. Most of them didn't have iceboxes and would send a child to get a pound of pan sausage for breakfast, or a loaf of bread, or a quart of syrup, things like that. When the first rush was over, they swept the store, got deliveries of new goods and restocked the shelves and vegetable bins, while Mr. Weaver went off to the packing house in his truck to pick up his fresh meat for the day. The Weavers didn't have a car, and Mr. Weaver or Wade drove the truck back and forth between the store and the house on Mildred Street.

Another rush of customers would come between ten and eleven o'clock in the morning. Afternoons were spent sacking up sugar and rice and dried peas and butter beans in the nickel or dime packages that were the most an ordinary customer would buy at one time. Late afternoon there was the big rush of the day, and the store closed at six or seven, depending on business. Hard times like those, people kept their stores open longer to take in what business they could.

I got to know all this because I was soon working there. I'd thought of asking Mr. Weaver for a job but didn't have the nerve. Hazel offered to ask for me, but I told her not to, she'd already done too much. Then one day we were both in the store, had already got what Hazel had come for, and were just standing around talking to Mr. Weaver when suddenly they got busy. Ten customers seemed to appear at once, and one little girl whose mother had sent her asked me for a ten-cent can of Bruton snuff. She thought I was a clerk because I was white and everybody else that worked there was white except Ed, and he was only the delivery boy.

Hazel said to me with a wink, "Get it for her; you know where things are." I did know, because of hanging around so much.

Mr. Weaver said, "Sure, help us out, Trudy."

So I did. I waited on people and took their money, but of course didn't use the cash register, only gave the money to Harvey or Mr. Weaver and let them ring up the amount and make change. The rush of customers built like it sometimes does, and it was half an hour before the store cleared out, by which time Hazel had gone home by herself. Mr. Weaver said, "I sure do thank you, Trudy. Now, the least I can do is set my new clerk up to a Coca-Cola." I accepted, but knowing he was being pleasant and not meaning it about my being the new clerk. However, I had my own ideas about that. I decided to wait a couple of days and ask him to let me work odd hours morning or afternoon they had more work than they could handle easily.

As it happened, luck was with me. Two days after that Harvey Miller came down with the mumps, which a lot of jokes were made about that I didn't understand until later. The first morning he didn't show up for work and his wife telephoned to say he was sick, Mr. Weaver sent Ed to Hazel's to ask if I could help him out. It was to be for just that day. He planned to have Wade stay out of school until Harvey got well, but it happened that Wade had a big English test next day he couldn't afford to miss, and the day after the band was playing for the ROTC to parade at some special inspection at Lanier. He came straight from school, though, every day and worked till closing time. Mr. Weaver offered to let me go home when things weren't busy, but I told him I'd rather stay right through. It made a long day, twelve or thirteen hours, and at first I got pretty tired, but I was soon used to it. I liked the activity and people coming and going. All I had to do for them to accept me as a clerk was to put on an apron. My being a girl didn't matter, although Mr. Weaver worried some about that at first. However, I was careful never to let it make any difference in what I did. I was strong, and I got stronger. I was accurate and quick at weighing up the small bags of

143

rice and sugar and dried things. I got to where I could
judge just how much to let slip into the bag from the scoop
without the scales, although I always used them, of course.
I learned where everything was and how to use the ladder
or the long rod with a hook on the end to topple things
from a high shelf I couldn't reach. I learned how to make
change from the cash register. I sold meat out of the case,
and before Harvey came back I even sometimes cut simple
things like neck bones and pork chops, or whacked spareribs down the middle with the cleaver just as well as anybody could. All I had to do was to do things right for Mr.
Weaver to begin taking my being there for granted. *Mrs.*
Weaver was another matter.

The first day I worked she came out on the bus to bring
Mr. Weaver his noon dinner, since he couldn't go home
for it as he usually did and leave me at the store by myself.
She stayed for three hours and even tried to help wait on
customers, but she didn't have the knack of it, and she
didn't know the stock. I knew she didn't like the idea of me
and Jim and had only grudgingly helped Jim get into
school, so I tried hard to do nothing she could fault. I took
the work seriously, and she soon saw that I did. When one
of the salesmen I recognized from the past came in to get
his order from Mr. Weaver, he made a joke that included
me, but I pretended not to understand. I'm sure Mrs.
Weaver worked on Mr. Weaver to let me go, but he
needed me; there was no one he could get he wouldn't have
to train, and I was picking up things pretty fast. By the
time he needed me less badly, everybody was used to my
being there. It was a month before Mrs. Weaver acknowl-
edged my presence in the store with more than a little nod
when she came in. She didn't come often; she wasn't one of
those women who interfered in their husband's business on

the pretense of helping; and I had an idea that both Mr. Weaver and Wade were careful not to mention me around home.

Harvey Miller didn't like my being there when he got well and came back, but there was nothing he could do about it. He tried to treat me as a joke, but I merely went about my work and didn't rise to his baiting. Aside from his teasing he was a good clerk, but he was lazy, and more and more, especially when Mr. Weaver's back was turned, he shifted some of his old jobs to me. I was putting away most of the new canned goods that came in—always taking the older cans out first so they could go in front. I soon did most of the weighing up and packaging of dried vegetables and fruit, of rice and sugar.

In those days flour was sold mostly in six- or twelve-pound cloth sacks. When these were delivered to the store they were shapeless and unmanageable. In order to stack them neatly they had to be beaten flat and firm with a wide wooden paddle kept for the purpose. That came to be my and Ed's job when he was between deliveries. We'd both be white as ghosts after an hour of such work, and Harvey would laugh and say he couldn't tell us apart, so we must be brother and sister. I don't think Ed liked that any more than I did.

The jobs I minded most were the ones like housework. One of those was cleaning glass with strong ammonia to get finger marks and grease spots off it. I hated the smell; it made my eyes and hands burn. In addition to the display case for meats, the glass of which had to be cleaned inside and out, there was a big glass case for candy and cigarettes, a few common cosmetics like talcum powder and Vaseline (much used to tame kinky hair) and medicines such as aspirin and Black Draught and castor oil. But the job I hated was cleaning the fish bins. They always stank and drew flies summer and winter, and the drains got clogged with fish scales.

Friday afternoon I sliced and weighed bacon in pound and half-pound packages. Saturday morning Wade and I killed and plucked chickens in the alley beyond the back door of the meat department. Ed helped us when he had time between delivering orders.

Though neither of us let on, Harvey and I never came to like one another. Some people I just don't like, can't like, and Harvey was one. He never did anything bad to me, but I even hated things about him like his gliding, sly walk and the way wiry black hair grew in tufts on the backs of his skinny fingers. The nearest to being directly nasty he ever got was to pass a coarse remark or joke now and then, if not to me directly then carefully in my hearing. This he never did when Wade or Mr. Weaver was there, but Wade was at school most of the time and Mr. Weaver had to go off in his truck two or three times a day on business to do with the store. It wasn't that Mr. Weaver or Wade treated me as anything special, but they were friendly and respected me, whereas Harvey despised me because of my situation in life. He was one of those poor men who had to hate anybody poorer than he was. I learned to ignore Harvey when he talked nasty; I pretended not to hear him. After all, what he said couldn't hurt me. The only thing he did that made me really mad was to call me "Sea Hag," a name he'd picked up from the comic strip "Popeye." When he did that, he made a big joke about it, but I didn't think it was funny and he knew I didn't.

Although I soon got used to the long hours, I'd get tired, especially on Saturday nights, when the store stayed open until nine o'clock. I'd go home to Hazel and Jim and we'd sit around the kitchen table drinking tea or milk and eating something good Hazel always saved for me. Mr. Harris was seldom there Saturdays and Sundays. Sometimes when I went to bed on Saturday night I cried with tiredness, not feeling sorry for myself, just aching, hurting *tired*. But that was cured by getting paid when we closed at one o'clock on Sunday. It was a happy time for everybody when Mr. Weaver paid us off: Harvey first, then Ed and me, then Wade. However hard the week had been, when I held in my hand the seven dollars I'd earned, I felt good; because, by God, it was mine.

CHAPTER 19

The store and Hazel's house were my life. Hazel got mad when I first tried to pay her five dollars a week for Jim and me, but when I pressed her and she had time to think about it, she agreed on four, although she said I ought to learn to be niggery and just take what was offered.

With my working at the store and Mr. Harris working on the railroad Hazel and Jim often found themselves keeping company. They'd go all over Montgomery, Hazel wearing her white uniform if she thought they'd run into objections. They went to parks and picture shows, to the First White House of the Confederacy and to the Museum, which Jim had heard about from Miss Kramer. Hazel was in no way, shape, form, or fashion a "mother" to either of us; she was Big Sister. She could be out of sorts, and when she was she made no effort to disguise what she felt, which encouraged us to speak our minds and to consult our own likes and dislikes, instead of showing a false face to the world. But, better than anyone else, she understood the border between honesty and consideration. She was a woman who enjoyed people. She hated hypocrisy and was hurt by the neighbors' ignoring her—for after their curiosity about Jim and me had made them unbend enough to ask who we were, they had gone back to snubbing Hazel.

Hazel was especially provoked by the behavior of a fat woman named Pearl Wigglesworth, who appeared to dominate the neighborhood women. Her face, dewlaps and all, was generally set in the grim look of one who saw Judgment Day ahead and knew that she alone would be let through the gate to sing with the blessed angels. She had never spoken to Hazel, but if Hazel passed her house when the woman was on her front porch, she would begin to sing a hymn. The hymns she favored were threatening; they promised death and damnation to the sinner who did not change his ways.

The first time we were sung at as we walked with Hazel past her house, Hazel did not change expression or look at the woman. But as soon as we got home, she raged.

"Hateful, fat sow! Singing her hymns at me! I could tell her what a wiggle's worth, and maybe one day I will! —You ought to see her leaving her church on a Sunday after service. Holds a pious look on her face careful as she'd carry an egg on a spoon. Her thoughts on the Lord, same time she's remembering to pull her dress out the crack of her ass. Oh my, one day I'm going to tell her; you wait."

Hazel's rages were short. "Reminds me. You shouldn't think the House down in New Orleans was all piano playing, and drinking home brew, and winking at the fellows come to have a good time. A lot of it we just sat around talking to kill time. Lot of things come out, lot of stories get told. Now, this 'un may and may not be true, I don't swear, but I hope for Pearl Wigglesworth's sake it is. One of our girls, Beatrice, told us how before she come to us she worked in a House in Galveston, Texas, where all the girls took names from hymns. She herself was called 'Joy to the World.' Another was 'Abide with Me.' And there was—" Hazel had begun to laugh, remembering the old time. "There was 'Amazing Grace'—wonder what she specialized in? And my favorite of all, 'Blest Be the Tie That Binds'!"

Selfishly, I liked it when Mr. Harris was away, because then I felt I was the man of the house, coming home from work to my friend Hazel and my brother Jim; and because I was the one that had worked long, they were obliging and generous to me. They hurried to tell me the events of their day, both talking at once, or one beginning a sentence and the other, or both, finishing it. Hazel shared Jim's first school days more than I could, because it was the new thing happening to them, whereas it seemed that a hundred things happened to me before noon and a thousand by nightfall. It was a period of fast growing for me. So was it for Jim, but each of us was self-absorbed.

Although I liked it better when Mr. Harris was not there, I knew Hazel missed him and looked to his return. When he was gone, she dimmed. It was like turning down the wick of a kerosene lamp. When he came back she burned bright. Mr. Harris was never quite real to me the way he was to Jim, the way he assuredly was to Hazel. I tended to see him as things that represented him when he wasn't there: a shirt Hazel washed and ironed, a pair of shoes Jim shined on the back doorsteps. (One of his thoughts was to pay Jim for small services, giving Jim a feeling of usefulness and independence.)

The fact was that I couldn't begin to figure Mr. Harris. Why did he not merely tolerate but encourage Hazel's keeping us? Because he saw that she needed someone when he was away, I told myself; but that did not satisfy me. I did not trust or accept his kindness, because I didn't understand it. Acceptance and rejection are mutual. Maybe Mr. Harris didn't accept me because I was female and white like the wife and daughters he clearly did not love, whereas he took to Jim because Jim was a boy, the son he hadn't had who might somehow have made his life different. Now and then he even called Jim "my boy" in a quick, quiet, joking way. I came to understand Mr. Harris better at a later time, but he was a puzzle to me then. Maybe I was jealous. I wanted Hazel for me and Jim, and I knew she put Mr. Harris first. Maybe too, I couldn't accept the fact of their sleeping together; if so, it had nothing to do with black and white, but with what had happened to me at the lumberyard. I was afraid of men.

Yet this fear did not extend to the store. The apron I wore said what I was; it set me apart the way any uniform will, and I needed that at the time. I respected Mr. Weaver. I despised Harvey but was careful with him. I felt nothing about Ed—nor did he about the rest of us, I might add. I found myself liking Wade, who didn't notice me much, but when he did, was nice. Although he worked cheerfully enough at the store, he was a serious boy; his mind was on school. He studied hard, and I soon learned that he wanted to go to college. Once in a while he mentioned Auburn in a hopeful way "if times ever get better." We worked well together. The main jobs we shared were bacon slicing and chicken killing. It was before Mr. Weaver bought an electric slicing machine, so Wade turned the handle, and I caught and placed the slices of bacon in orderly rows on wax paper. We got to where we could slice and package two sides of bacon in an hour, if nobody bothered us.

On Saturday morning Wade would build a fire in the alley under a big can of water set on bricks. I'd hold the feet and wings of a chicken and Wade would plunge the point of the knife through its head, which he held against a telephone pole. It was the quickest way to kill them. Sometimes we sang as we dipped the carcasses into the can of boiling water and plucked them, common songs like "Row, Row, Row Your Boat" and "Juanita," depending on whether we needed a lively song for cold weather or a slower one for a warm day.

CHAPTER 20

The first Saturday in December I thought I had a secret. I smiled to myself as I waited on customers and went about my normal work. It was a sunny, cold, blowy day. Wade had trouble keeping the fire around the water can when we were killing chickens; and old Pop Enoch, the neighborhood drunk, was sleeping it off in the alley and kept rolling closer and closer to the fire trying to stay warm. We were afraid he'd set himself on fire or tip the boiling water over himself, so we had to keep a watch on him.

Hazel sent Jim with my noon dinner in a basket, all as usual. Weekdays I went home for dinner, home being close, but on Saturdays we stayed so busy everybody ate at work, Mrs. Weaver bringing Wade's and Mr. Weaver's dinner, and Harvey making out on sardines and crackers because his wife June worked Saturdays in a beauty parlor giving manicures. We didn't eat supper till we went home, but around five o'clock Mr. Weaver sent Ed across the street to Callie's Cafe for a plate of hamburgers everybody except Ed shared, each paying for what he ate. They were a dime apiece, steaming hot, peppery, and dripping with grease. Ed had also bought four pig ear sandwiches. They were a nickel apiece; he said he'd rather have four of them than the two hamburgers I allowed myself.

Business built around six o'clock. The front door was constantly opening and closing with customers coming and going. The air was soft with floating layers of cigarette smoke, and the radio on a back shelf blared out the Saturday night programs. Many people, particularly the older men, came into the store not to buy anything but to stand and talk and hear the radio. Business was over by eight o'clock, and Mr. Weaver closed the store a little before nine. He and Wade and Harvey got into the truck and Wade drove off. Ed creaked away on his bicycle, and I walked down Day Street toward Hazel's. Callie's Cafe was still open, and the houses I passed had lamps burning. There wasn't much car traffic, and the people on the street walked fast, hands in their pockets, the breath of their words making steam because it was cold weather. Music came from one of the houses. Somebody was playing a scratchy record of "Bully of the Town."

I pushed my hands deeper into my sweater pockets, and my left thumb commenced to throb. I'd tied a kerosene rag around it yesterday after cutting it on the blade of the bacon slicer, reaching too fast. Turning off Day Street I lifted my head because the wind was less strong and I was almost home. Then I stopped in my tracks. Hazel's house was dark. Since I had known it, I had never seen it so.

Mounting to the porch I touched the door cautiously, expecting I don't know what to jump out at me, and it swung open. I stepped in, but as I reached for the wall switch to turn on the lights, a hand gripped my arm. I froze for the seconds before Jim giggled and turned on the lights himself.

Hazel was holding my arm. "*Now*, Jim!" she said.

As she continued to hold me, Jim began to spank me on the butt hard as he could swing, counting as he hit. "One! Two! Three! Four! Five! Six! Seven! Eight! Nine! Ten! Eleven! Twelve! Thirteen! Fourteen! And one to grow on!"

"Happy birthday, Trudy!" Hazel said. And Jim said, "Happy birthday!"

"How did you know?" I accused them.

"I'm a mind reader, a gypsy fortune-teller!" Hazel said.

"I told her, Smarty!" Jim bragged.

"Smarty yourself, how did you remember?"

"Jim," Hazel said, "you go do what I said do. Holler when you ready."

He ran out toward the kitchen. "Take your sweater off," Hazel said. "You look like Marie Dressler in that *Anna Christie.*"

Presently Jim shouted, "Come on, I'm ready!" and we went to find him in the kitchen. As we got to the door he switched off the ceiling light. On the center of the big table was a cake with white icing and fourteen lighted pink candles set into pink candy rosettes like I'd seen once at a birthday party back in Pluma.

"Make a wish and blow them out!" Hazel said. "You make a wish too, Jim."

"Can I wish for me?" he said.

She cuffed him. "For *her*, old Selfish! We shall wish together for Trudy."

I wished and blew hard, and as the last candles flickered out, Hazel turned on the ceiling light and we looked at the smoking white cake. I didn't say anything.

Hazel said, "I bet you hungry. *I* am, and Jim always is." She went to the stove and brought back a platter covered with another platter upside down. Removing the top one she revealed a stack of fried mullet. Jim brought a plate of thin corn bread from the stove, where it had been left to keep warm. "Jim, get the ketchup," Hazel said.

Jim did, from the refrigerator, and we sat down and ate. When we got to cutting the cake, Hazel opened a door of the kitchen cabinet and brought out three packages wrapped in pretty paper.

"While we eat cake," she said, "you open your presents." She studied the three before handing me one. Jim looked disappointed. "This one first," she said. "From Mr. Harris."

I unwrapped the layers of thin white tissue paper to find a string of blue beads. It was my first piece of jewelry, and Hazel fastened it around my neck and went to get her looking glass so I could see myself. "The clasp is fourteen-carat gold," she said.

All the time Jim was looking anxious and important, so when Hazel handed me the next package, she said, "This is from Big Jim over there."

I untied the ribbon instead of forcing it off and opened the wrapping paper to find a book. It was a copy of Walt Whitman's *Leaves of Grass*.

"I bought it on Perry Street at the Booklovers Shop," Jim said. "She said it was a book everybody had to read sooner or later. Do you like it?"

I told him I did, and I did, knowing what it must have meant to Jim to spend his own money on a present for anybody. I have it still, and I treasure it, although I have never read more than a dozen pages of it.

"Here. Last like the cow's tail." Hazel shoved the third gift to me.

It was a bottle of perfume. I opened it and smelled it. I had smelled perfume before—Hazel's, and, long ago, Mama's when she had some. But this was mine, not just a dab on a handkerchief from somebody else's bottle, but a whole bottle of perfume for Trudy Maynard. Hazel was watching me, and I saw she knew what it meant.

Jim yawned and asked if he could have another piece of cake.

"You're a greedy-gut," Hazel said. "I think I'll have another piece too. Nobody loves a hungry whore. That's a saying."

CHAPTER 21

The history books tell us that was the worst winter of the Depression. It should have been a gloomy Christmas, but it wasn't. Even on Day Street people managed to find a scrap of bread and a scrape of grease to soften it.

Times were hard and might get worse before getting better, but Franklin D. Roosevelt was going to be President next March, and everybody made up his mind to last until then. Meantime, eat scraps. Children craving sweets would find a candy wrapper on the sidewalk and open it and press it to their faces in ecstasies at the sweet smell. Frail men, too proud to beg and too old to work even if there had been jobs, came to the store in their best, clean, mended clothes, because the store was where food was, although they had no money to buy it. Without any seeming indication on either side, there would be an understanding between an old man and Mr. Weaver. Smiling and saying little, but that with the most perfect courtesy, Mr. Weaver would cut off and wrap a piece of salt pork, or crack a few spareribs or neck bones and wrap them and hand them to one of the men. To be sure, it wasn't much, but a man with a package of meat in his hand had his pride intact and would be welcome in somebody's kitchen.

Hazel kept as busy as a cat moving kittens in a flood. She sent Christmas cards to all the girls in the House in New Orleans. She shopped Downtown for presents. She put on her white uniform and went to the Sayre Street School to watch Jim be a shepherd in a pageant that drew its participants from the first four grades. She made fudge and divinity candy and gave Jim a box of both mixed for Miss Kramer. She bought and hung red and green streamers. The house was full of red paper bells she bought flat and opened out. She bought holly and a big pine tree on the Tuesday after my birthday. Then she and Jim spent two days decorating it. We went to sleep with the smell of pine and woke to it.

"Love pine," I can hear her saying. "It may not have the regular shape of others, but I don't care nothing about that. If there's heaven and not just hell the way Pearl Wigglesworth wants it, it'll smell of pine trees."

Mr. Harris provided a special treat by borrowing a car for the two days he was with us just before Christmas. Although he and Hazel never walked out together, they figured that in a car, with me and Jim or sometimes just Jim if I was working, they could be seen together without causing comment. As Hazel said, "Anybody see us can just say to himself, he's taking the cook home." They drove all over everywhere, into the country to buy fresh cane syrup and homemade sausage and pecans, and through the residential streets of Montgomery to see the private Christmas decorations. That was before such decorations became so elaborate as to seem silly. People prettied up their houses in simpler ways: live wreaths on the front door, small paper ones attached to the draw cord of window shades, Christmas trees set by a window so people passing would see them. And of course there were the store windows Downtown full of things we didn't want but loved to look at.

Hazel bought coconuts, punched holes in the eyes with her ice pick so Jim and I could drink the milk, then cracked the coconuts with a brick on the back doorstep and set Jim to grating the white meat for ambrosia. She kept a big cut-glass bowl full of ambrosia, saying she'd never had enough of it in her life. It was made with fresh oranges and bananas and canned pineapple and cherries—and the coconut Jim kept reminding all of us he had grated.

Mr. Harris wasn't there on Christmas Day. He had to make his run back to New Orleans and spend it with his wife and two daughters and their husbands. But he had looked glum enough at the prospect to satisfy Hazel, and after he left she gave her entire attention to me and Jim. It was the best Christmas we ever had. Jim's big present was roller skates and an Indian suit, for which he had expressed a strong preference over a cowboy suit, in spite of his enthusiasm for George O'Brien. Mine was two new dresses, a wool and a silk, Hazel had made without my knowing a thing about them from patterns she'd cut before. She also gave me my first pair of real silk stockings in the shade they called Gun Metal.

We had both given Mr. Harris a box of handkerchiefs, and he was nice enough to say nobody ever had too many. Jim gave Hazel bath salts and talcum powder in a set, and I gave her a framed picture of an old-fashioned ship under sail against a beautiful sunset. They had done it so it would look like a real oil painting. She hung it over the sofa in the living room, saying, "We used to have a lot of pictures on the walls of the House, but believe me they were nothing like this."

Then it was 1933.

Jim said, "This is the year I'll be *eight years old!*"

"I'll be fifteen," I said.

"Why do you always have to be biggety?" he said. "Anyway, I'll be eight on April twenty-seventh, and you won't be fifteen for nearly a whole year."

"Jim," I said, "sometimes you give me a pain I can't locate."

"Well," Hazel temporized, "if you see anything you never saw before, throw a stick at it. That's my motto. Jim, you like me to pass you some more black-eyed peas?" We were having the traditional New Year's Day dinner of hog's head and black-eyed peas. It was supposed to cleanse the system of heavy Christmas indulgences.

Jim took another helping of peas and added a spoonful of piccalilli to them, stirring the whole mess together.

Hazel, who had been studying to herself with her eyes nearly closed, said to me, "You think Mr. Harris looks peaky?"

"No," I said, "he looks like he always does." The truth was I seldom looked directly at Mr. Harris in a thinking way.

She pushed her chair back. "Time to take down the Christmas tree. When Christmas is over, it's over."

CHAPTER 22

Harvey hogged the adding machine. Because of that and my country ignorance of machinery, I seldom used it. No matter how long the line of figures when I had a customer who bought a lot, I added them with my pencil. Harvey really considered the adding machine his. He was the chief clerk and spent more time waiting on customers than Mr. Weaver or Wade did, and I didn't count.

As I wrote down my figures on the unopened paper bag and he jabbed his on the adding machine, he would spare me a glance that was tolerant and superior in the same way somebody riding looks at somebody walking. When he thought he could get by with it, he cheated a customer.

This is how he did it.

If he was adding up a big order and the customer was standing there, he would pretend to make a mistake on the machine and tear the used paper off the top. But he would not clear the machine before he started adding again, and the "mistake" he had made was one with a zero at the end after the decimal point. Even if a customer added up his bill when he got home, assuming that he kept the bill and could add, he might stop short of checking it thoroughly if the last column was correct. I didn't find this out by spying on Harvey; he told me. Harvey couldn't resist trying to show me he was smarter than other people. That led me to wonder what happened to the money he got by cheating. Did it become the store's or did it find a way to Harvey's pocket? He never told the Weavers about that trick of his; that I knew.

One Saturday we were waiting on customers and using the same counter. We happened to be adding figures about the same time, and the orders happened to be about the same size. I added mine up and flipped open the bag to put the groceries inside while Harvey still tapped and jabbed away at the adding machine. Wade was standing by. He suddenly laughed and said, "Harvey, I believe Trudy can add faster without the machine than you can with it."

Harvey looked surprised and his face turned red, but he also managed to suggest with a shrug that he knew Wade was just trying to make me feel good. Mr. Weaver came out of the meat department just then, wiping his hands on his stained apron, and Wade repeated what he had said.

Mr. Weaver said, "I'm slow on that machine myself. Seems to me more trouble than it's worth."

Harvey was in command of himself by then. Laughing, he gave me a little shove, pretending it was in fun. "She's a smart one, all right," he said. "But you don't really pretend you're faster than me, do you, Trudy?"

"Tell you," Wade said. "Let's have a race."

Often enough they played a little game like that when there was a lull in trade, the game usually started by Harvey. It was a way to break the monotony of the long day we worked, and Mr. Weaver never minded as long as it didn't interfere with business.

Wade tore off two strips of butcher paper from a big roll and quickly jotted down the same set of figures on both, telling us what he was doing but writing so we couldn't see the figures until he was done. Then, handing the strips to us, he said, "Ready? Go!"

I worked as fast as I could because I wanted to beat Harvey, and I did. I finished and handed the paper to Wade.

"She beat you!" Wade said.

Harvey worked on till he finished and totaled his columns on the adding machine, then tore the slip off and said slyly, "I had to set down the figures. They were already set down for her."

"Yeah, but she had to add them, and the machine did that for you," Wade said.

"Let's see if she made any mistakes," Harvey said, and took my paper from Wade's hand. "Look," he said after comparing it to his. "She added the whole thing wrong—so much for her being fast!"

Wade took my sheet of figures, automatically cleared the adding machine the way anyone does who wants to be sure of getting an accurate account, copied the original figures off and totaled them. Checking the sum against mine, he said, "She's right. Yours must be wrong."

"Maybe you're both wrong." Harvey tried his bluffing laugh.

Wade had taken up Harvey's account. After studying it he said, "You punched the wrong figure here."

Harvey looked at it. "I thought this nine was a seven. Looks like a seven, you have to admit."

By then a customer had come in and I had gone to wait on her, and the telephone had rung and Mr. Weaver had gone to answer it, so the game petered out.

But Mr. Weaver didn't forget it. I could tell he was noticing the way I worked the next few days, and the following week he began to involve me in what he called his bookwork. Pretty soon I was helping every evening before we closed with the day's bookkeeping. I think Wade had spoken to him at home. Neither Wade nor Mr. Weaver had any leaning toward bookkeeping, and it turned out that I did, although I'd never thought of such a thing when I was going to school and hadn't been especially good at arithmetic. Mr. Weaver didn't keep good records, I soon could tell, just how much cash came in and how much went out, with little or no reference to the credit he gave people or credit wholesalers gave him. He didn't even keep a written record of the changes in the wholesale price of goods, but said he "carried all that in his head." He seemed glad if everything came out more or less even when he'd paid all his bills.

Wade took the general course at Lanier High School, but a girl he sometimes dated took the commercial course, and he brought me one of the old textbooks she had already used in a bookkeeping class. At first I could make little of it, but after studying awhile one thing would come clear for me, and that would lead to another. By the middle of February I was doing most of the store's bookwork. I don't mean to suggest I had mastered bookkeeping in that time, but I was keeping a better record of the money and stock than Mr. Weaver had done before. I had also begun to examine the charge accounts. There were two big ledgers of them, with the dead accounts—those no longer active, which Mr. Weaver had little hope of collecting payment on—mixed with the active accounts.

Wade was pleased to see me working on the books, feeling rightly that he had started it all, however accidentally. Mr. Weaver never praised me, but he did something better; he raised me to eight dollars a week.

CHAPTER 23

Although Hazel and I never saw Mr. Harris in his working clothes, Jim did. Jim had begged to see the engine, so one morning when he was leaving on his run, Mr. Harris said, "All right, boy, come on." It was a school holiday because somebody big had died. Off he and Jim went, and Jim was to come home on the bus by himself. He did, but when I went home at noon to have dinner with him and Hazel, he was mighty quiet about it.

At our prodding he said that yes, Mr. Harris had changed into overalls and denim coat and then he had showed him the engine.

Hazel laughed, shaking her head. "Can't see that man in

overalls—just don't suit him. What else? Tell about the engine."

"Nothing to tell," Jim said.

"Jim, you are the most provoking boy!" she said. "You can talk ninety to the minute about Miss Kramer said this and how Eddie Cantor rolls his eyes, but something I want to know about— Did he show you how the engine worked?"

"Yes," Jim said, "but I didn't follow that so good."

"Most boys would be thrilled to death to go over a locomotive engine like that and have it all explained. Why aren't you?" Jim wouldn't look at her. "Now, what's the matter?" she pressed him.

Still not looking at her or me he mumbled, "I was scared of it."

That at least relieved Hazel. She relaxed and let him alone to eat his dinner.

If the trip to look at the engine hadn't worked out so well, other trips Jim and Mr. Harris made together worked fine. They even came back from a cattle show claiming they had enjoyed it. Hazel knew Mr. Harris liked taking Jim around with him, and she didn't like to see either one of them sit around the house too much, so she encouraged their excursions, saying, "You-all go do something for an hour or two. I got some sewing that won't wait." Or there was something special she wanted to cook and she didn't want them walking in and out of her kitchen distracting her. Or she wanted to work in her garden in the back yard. It was already blooming with spring flowers, and Hazel took great pride and pleasure in it at that time.

So when he wasn't in school, Jim and Mr. Harris—"my menfolks" as Hazel referred to them—went about town together. Jim got him to see Fredric March in *Dr. Jekyll and Mr. Hyde*. Afterwards they went to Kress to have a chocolate milk shake and Mr. Harris bought Jim a chemistry set. Jim was an awful pain to watch pouring things from one tumbler into another.

I worked a full day every day, but Mr. Weaver was good to me. Now and then he'd say, "Trudy, why don't you take a few hours off? Go Downtown and see a picture show or go shopping. They tell me girls always have a lot of things they want to buy at Kress or Woolworth. You can be back in time for the late rush."

I didn't like doing it, because I thought he was just treating me like a girl and it was important to me to work as hard as any of them did. But I gradually got to taking a little time off from the store when he suggested it, because he pointed out I was doing all the bookwork now, and he knew I carried some of it home to do. Of course, none of this sat well with Harvey. I had to put up with and learn to ignore a lot of heavy teasing about "our little bookkeeper."

Although I had enough on my mind, I hadn't forgot what Hazel had said at Christmas about Mr. Harris looking "peaky." She was right. He did. Ever since I'd known him he'd been a skinny man, but I began to look at him closer after her remark, and I could see his color was bad. Hazel didn't say any more to me about him, but I could tell she was worried, the way she looked at him when she was sure he wasn't looking at her. He began to take a nap almost every afternoon, Jim told me, and Hazel would lie down with him, although I'd heard her say she hated to go to bed in the daytime, having spent so much of her life doing it. Then, happening to glance at him one night when we were all sitting in the living room listening to the radio, I saw a look in his eyes that reminded me of Mama not long before she died.

CHAPTER 24

One afternoon soon after Mr. Weaver had raised me to eight dollars a week I had a telephone call from Mrs. Weaver.

"Trudy!"

"Yes, ma'am?"

"Something awful has happened! —This woman came, said she was a checker of some kind working for the Board of Education and she'd like to see Mrs. Maynard, James Maynard's mother, if she was home. I said she was but she was an invalid and never left her room and never saw anybody except her family and the doctor. She asked me to find out if she could talk to her just for a minute, even through the door, and I said no, it was out of the question, she couldn't possibly. I said Mrs. Maynard was never to be disturbed, it was a nervous disorder with complications, the doctor had specifically said so. —I felt terrible saying that! I think I said too much. I could see she didn't believe me, though she stayed polite. I regret the day I ever let Hazel Fay talk me into such a thing. I never tell lies, and I'm most upset about it."

"I'm sorry, Mrs. Weaver," I said. "Indeed I am, and very much obliged to you, me and Jim both—"

"Well, I'm sorry too. I regret ever saying I'd say something that wasn't true; I don't know what got into me to make such a promise. But Hazel Fay said probably nobody would ever ask me anyway, and if they hadn't, it would have been only *her* telling them a lie about where Jim lived and not my fault. You see?"

"Yes, ma'am. Do you think the lady will come back?"

"I just don't know. She looked thoughtful when she left. I do know that if she comes back, I can't lie to her again, I'll have to tell her the truth."

"Did she say why she'd come after all this time?" I asked.

"No, she didn't. Yes, she did. —I can't think, I'm so upset about this whole thing. But she did say something about their getting a telephone call from somebody saying they ought to investigate where James Maynard lived because—oh, I don't know. I was more concerned about what I was saying to her than what she was saying to me!"

I tried to soothe her down, but I'm never easy on the telephone because I hate talking to somebody I can't see. She kept interrupting me until finally she talked herself quieter and said good-by and then how was business today and hung up without waiting for me to answer. One of the last things she'd said stuck in my head. "Who could have told them to check on Jim?"

Putting the receiver back on the hook I looked across the store at Harvey. There were no customers in the store. Mr. Weaver had gone off in the truck. Wade was in school. Harvey went to the soft-drinks box and took out a Dr. Pepper and opened it. He sometimes treated himself, and he sometimes forgot to write it down against his account if nobody was there but him and me. When I left the telephone and went back to weighing up rice in the six-ounce bags we sold for a nickel, he sidled over and squinted at the scales as if to see that I was doing it right. His breath had a carbonated cherry smell from the Dr. Pepper. I sneezed. He belched.

The gentle old German farmer who grew such fine cabbages came in with his daughter, and I stopped weighing rice. Her name was Gertrude too, and she made sauerkraut like they don't put in cans.

Harvey immediately began to tease Mr. Kurz and imitate his accent. The old man always took it good-naturedly, but I knew it bothered Gertrude, so I drew her aside to talk. She was two years older than I, with streaky blond hair that became a fashion thirty years later and coarse brown skin from being out in all weather. Her mother was dead, and she had no brothers. She and her father worked the truck farm together.

Then Ed came back from making a delivery, and right after him Mr. Weaver drove up. He and Mr. Kurz were friendly and after they greeted each other, Mr. Kurz put his arm around Mr. Weaver's shoulders and took him off to his truck to look at some eggs and chickens he wanted to sell, both of them ignoring Harvey. Gertrude (I never

called her anything else, although she called me Trudy)
smiled at that. We felt the same way about Harvey. He
slipped his Dr. Pepper bottle into a slot of the case for
empties and wandered into the meat department like he
had more important things to do than talk to us.

Mrs. Weaver's visit from the Board of Education lady
stayed on my mind, but it wasn't repeated, and gradually I
felt relieved. Also, March 4 came, bringing the event that
was to change all of our lives: Franklin D. Roosevelt was
inaugurated as President of the United States. To celebrate
it there was a big parade Downtown on Dexter Avenue.
Mr. Weaver insisted that I take two hours off and go to the
parade with Hazel, and I'm glad I did, because it was a
sight to behold. There were bands playing, and the American Legion marched, as did the Elks Club, the Kiwanis,
and others; as, in fact, did just about every schoolchild,
black or white, in town.

We saw Wade, stepping out like a real soldier in his
ROTC uniform with the Lanier band. Finally, here came
Jim's class, with Jim looking as good as anybody, walking
right beside Miss Kramer and waving his American flag
with the other children. All of them were singing "Happy
Days Are Here Again."

Jim didn't see us. After they'd passed, Hazel kept patting
me on the back, her face shining. "Everything's going to be
all right! Mr. Roosevelt is up there in the White House in
Washington, D.C., and *everything's* going to be all right!"

CHAPTER 25

I didn't think about it until it happened, but the important thing when I saw Aunt Olive again was that I was no longer afraid. I didn't run as I had with Jim after catching a glimpse of her in Woolworth's that other time. It's what living with Hazel and working at the store had done for me.

It was eleven-thirty on Thursday of the week following Inauguration Day and the parade. As she came into the store, she might have been returning from church on the Sunday she'd left me exact instructions on what time to start cooking dinner, only to find me nodding in my chair, the work not begun. She looked just the same, as respectable as a clean handkerchief and as ugly as a scab with pus under it.

"So there you are!"

The late morning rush of business was over. Mr. Weaver was opening a Wisconsin cheese on the butcher block he'd just scraped clean with his wire brushes. Harvey was looking busier than he was, opening cases of tinned yellow and bottled black snuff. I had just used a crowbar to pry the top off an orange crate and was removing the tissue from oranges on the first layer. Each tissue wrapping was stamped with the trade name and symbol "Blue Goose" and I had opened one flat to study it. I looked at her and didn't say a word.

"Gertrude!" she said in a tone that once would have made me jump.

"Yes, ma'am?"

"What are you doing here?"

"I work for Mr. Weaver," I said. "He owns Weaver's Market." Then I said automatically, not meaning to be smart, "What can I do for you?"

"You can tell me why you suddenly disappeared! —Took your brother and ran away leaving me—leaving all of us to come home to a cold stove and Sunday dinner not even started!"

I had been right, that Sunday dinner still rankled in her mind. "How do you happen to be here, Aunt Olive?"

Harvey stayed quietly busy, but Mr. Weaver left the cheese on the meat block and came over.

"I was advised by—I will not name the source of my information because—" She continued talking, but I did not follow her words. My mind was taken with an image of Harvey Miller working the snuff out of my sight, busy as a

squirrel storing acorns for winter. I hadn't told Harvey
much about Jim and me, but I had talked some to Wade
and Mr. Weaver, and Hazel was no one to make a secret of
anything. "—and so I came to see for myself. I couldn't
believe it. Is it true too that you're living out here? Living
with Nigras? —I might add that the information I've just
received wasn't the first clue I had. There was the Inauguration Parade. Lucien marched in it, and my precious Alice
rubbed a blister on her left heel wearing new shoes she
refused to go to the parade without. They both said they
thought they saw your brother and that he was with a
bunch of children from another school—"

"Sayre Street Grammar," I said. "Aunt Olive, this is Mr.
Weaver; I work for him."

"And she's a big help," Mr. Weaver said, willing as
always to be friendly. "It was my lucky day when she
showed up."

"Mr. Weaver, this is my Aunt Olive Anderson. You
remember my mentioning them."

"Glad to meet you, ma'am," he said politely. "Trudy, if
you want to take a little time off to have a talk with your
aunt, that'll be all right with me."

"Thank you, sir," I said. "That might be best. I'll be
back soon."

She couldn't let that by. "I'm not sure you'll be back at
all. You come right out to my car. I'm parked across the
street."

I followed her but kept my apron on. The car was in
front of Callie's Cafe, and Callie was standing at the door.
"How's the world treating you, Trudy?" she said.

"Not so bad," I said. "How you feel this morning?"

"I got a kind of ache in my gut. Must have been eating
my own cooking!" She laughed heartily.

"Gertrude, get in this car," Aunt Olive said.

Callie went back into the cafe. I slid onto the front seat by Aunt Olive, but left the door partly open, even though it was the traffic side. It was the first time I'd been in that car. Aunt Olive frowned hard at me. "You've grown," she said, making it an accusation.

"I've been eating regular."

"You're showing yourself off too much," she said. "Up there," she added in case I hadn't understood.

"That's God's work, Aunt Olive, with a little help from Hazel's cooking."

"Is she the Nigra woman you and your brother live with?"

"Yes, ma'am."

"She's a whore and lives with a white man," she said in a way calculated to throw me off balance.

"She's our friend and *we* live with her. Mr. Harris comes to visit when he's in town."

"You needn't try any tricky way of putting it to me. I'm told she's just a common Nigra whore."

"Hazel says there are two things you can't keep people from doing if they mix together: they'll fight and they'll fuck."

She slapped me, but only a glancing blow because of the confined space. "Don't you dare use filthy language to me!"

"I'll use worse if you call Hazel any more names. Who told you about her? Harvey Miller?"

"Who told me shall be nameless. I will not betray a trust."

"Harvey can't stand me because I'm smarter than he is."

That upset her more than what I'd said before. She turned full in the front seat, her elbow hitting the horn on the steering wheel. Callie, obviously curious about me and the stranger, came back to stand in her doorway. "I don't give curb service," she joked. "Are you all right, Trudy?" I nodded to her.

"They seem to consider you one of themselves," Aunt Olive said, "and I'm sure you're no better than they are. You're even more biggety and independent than when you left my house!"

"A lot of things have happened since we left your house," I said, "including us going hungry and getting beat up, and my being raped."

"By a Nigra? Merciful stars! Was it a Nigra?"

"No, it was a white tramp in a lumberyard."

"You've sunk even lower than I thought you would," she said with satisfaction.

"Nothing that's happened to us was as bad as staying in your house; I want you to know that, Aunt Olive."

"You need not think you'll have the opportunity to do so again. My duty is clear. I'm going to tell your uncle everything you've said to me. I'm sure he'll agree that the only thing to do with you is turn you over to the authorities. You won't be going to a nice Home either, like the one your uncle took the trouble to arrange for you before. You'll go to reform school, where I hope they whip and shame some humility into you."

I opened the car door full and stepped over to the sidewalk.

She leaned out from back of the steering wheel. "Are you trying to run away again?"

"No, ma'am, I'm not running anywhere. I'm going back to work."

"Make the best of it, for it may well be your last day of

freedom. I'll see that you go to jail for what you've said to me!"

Callie stepped down from her doorway to the sidewalk beside me. "You sure you don't need help, Trudy?"

"Mind your own business, woman!" Aunt Olive shouted at her.

I said to Callie, "I was just having a talk with my aunt."

Callie gave Aunt Olive a big, knowing smile. "You're the lady had the goldfish! Jim and Hazel told me about that. Lawd-a-mercy!"

Aunt Olive slammed her foot on the starter. "Your uncle will tend to you!"

She was gone.

CHAPTER 26

Uncle Earl came that night. He parked his car near the store and waited until we closed and I started down Day Street before he stepped out and spoke to me. I shied, more nervous than surprised after Aunt Olive's threats. But he put his hand on my arm in so mild a way I said, "Good evening, Uncle Earl," and waited for him to say what he'd come for.

"You want to get in the car so we can talk?"

"No, sir. I've been in that car one time today. We can both say what we have to right here, if you don't mind." Most of Day Street was indoors having supper if there was supper to be had, so there were few people passing. We could see each other clear enough. We weren't exactly under a streetlight, but there was one nearby.

"Well." He looked around uncomfortably. "Olive told me what you said to her."

"Did she tell you what she said to me?"

"Enough for me to fill in and use my imagination." I glanced at him. It was the first time I'd heard anything in his voice or sensed anything in his attitude toward Aunt Olive like a comment—I won't say criticism.

"She bad-mouthed my friend Hazel Fay."

"The colored woman that took you in?" he said.

"Yes, sir."

"How long after you left our house did you go to hers?"

I told him.

"Why did you run away like that, you and your brother?"

I said, "It was better than going to a Home. If we'd let you put us there, it would have been giving up. —Also, we were afraid they'd separate us. It's not that we're so crazy about each other, but he's the closest I've got."

For a wonder, he nodded as if he understood. Then he swallowed a couple of times, not finding his next question easy. "What happened to you between the time you left us and went to this—?"

"Hazel Fay."

"Well then, Hazel Fay."

I told him most of it, briefly but not leaving out anything important, only trying to spare his male sensibilities.

"My God," he said, and touched me on the shoulder. I drew away, despising him for his sympathy. He looked uncomfortable. "Then that colored girl taunted you, you say, and told you to 'go to the whore's house'?"

"That's what she said," I agreed, having only just told him the words she used.

"And she took you in like that? Why?"

"She wasn't going to, but then she noticed Jim was bruised and his face had a cut. She didn't mean to let us stay, but it kept raining all that day—" I stopped, unable to explain it so that it would make sense to him.

"One thing led to another," he said.

"That's right," I said. "That's the way it was." I told him about Mr. Harris, how old he was, and that he was the only one who ever came to the house. I didn't say he had a wife and family in New Orleans, just that he was a railroad man and therefore in and out of town. He listened, not saying anything but nodding now and then to show he was following me. When I stopped, we stood there on the dirt sidewalk facing each other but not looking directly at each other. A little boy everybody called Sugar, not because he was sweet but because he had a great craving for it, came running along.

"Hey, Trudy!" he said.

"Hey, Sugar!" I said.

"Can't stop! I'm in a big hurry!"

When he'd gone, I shifted my feet, wanting to get on home to supper, but Uncle Earl was still doing some thinking. "So then you began to eat regular, and she made new clothes for you. And Jim started to school. And you got yourself this job at the store." I nodded. "In fact, you did what you'd wanted to do and we wouldn't let you do."

I wouldn't fudge. "Yes, sir. I'm not blaming anybody."

"Now all you want us to do is leave you alone."

My not answering was the answer.

He frowned and thought. "Of course, I don't like to see you living out here with these"—he swallowed and skipped the word—"around, but I can't offer you anything better, and it looks to me like it's up to you where you live and what you do."

Simple though it was, his saying that was a weight off my mind. "If you could make Aunt Olive just forget about us."

"I can't make her do anything," he said gloomily, "but I'll try." Uncle Earl was one of those who, the more he said, the harder it was to put trust in him. "I think maybe I can. I'll certainly try to think of something to tell her that will keep her still."

"She's pretty strong against us," I said.

"I know it. You don't understand your Aunt Olive. It's because she's concerned about you and your brother. You probably haven't thought much about this Depression, but she sees you as a threat, to take away from Alice and Lucien."

"Tell her we don't want a thing they've got."

He looked at me with surprise. "Well, it looks to me like you're not doing so bad for yourself. You must think I haven't been much use, much of an uncle to you."

"I don't know that kinfolks have to shiver together under the same quilt," I said.

"Well. If I can ever help you in any way—" He stopped, remembering he'd said something like that the time he brought Mama's tombstone to Pluma. He cleared his throat to get past his embarrassment.

"Show me where you live. I don't mean I want to go in, but if I could tell Olive I've seen it. I promise I won't go in."

I led us down Day Street and we turned off toward Hazel's house. As we passed Pearl Wigglesworth's porch, she was coming out her door. Seeing us she clapped her hands and said, "Lord-God-Jesus, another one!"

Uncle Earl looked wondering. "She's just crazy," I said.

There was a light in the living room and the shades were up, but since nobody was to be seen, I figured Hazel and Jim were back in the kitchen getting supper ready. Mr. Harris was away on his run. We weren't expecting him until Monday.

Uncle Earl peered through the windows. "It's certainly no ordinary nigger house," he decided. I bristled but didn't say anything. "In fact, it looks very decent." He turned back to me. "I don't want to lose touch with you-all, because of your Mama, you know. If anything—I mean, you wouldn't have to bother your Aunt Olive, you could phone me at the office."

"Yes, sir," I said, and went into the house.

The smell of frying ham hit me as I opened the front door, and when I got to the kitchen, Jim was reading slowly out loud as Hazel turned the slices in the pan. "Uh-huh," she said to him. "Now go back to the start and read straight through so it all runs together. Sometimes you're so slow I forget the connection between the last thing and the next. —You a little late, Trudy. Go wash if you want to, then listen to Jim's story book till I take up. It's about a boy had a dog named Jack."

That's the way it happened, or the way I remember it. I could despise Uncle Earl, but I couldn't really hate him any more. A true villain is a source of satisfaction if he becomes the focus of fear, a fixed point for all the hob-goblins that sleep by day and keep us from sleep at night. But let a villain slip into understanding, and he is lost. It's easier to lose a friend than a true villain.

CHAPTER 27

Some secret knowledge must work to prepare us, for people's looks often begin to alter before the event we later look back on and say, "That brought the change." It was so with Hazel. By April it was hot, and she worked hour after hour at her garden in the back yard. She dug, she weeded, she watered, she staked. She couldn't work herself hard enough. It was as though she was afraid to stop, because if she did, the big *It* would catch her; so she had to run and keep on running.

Coming home around noon one day for dinner, I found her still working in the broiling sun. When I called to her from the back door, she came and sat on the steps. She'd been working without a hat. Her dress stuck to her showing a boniness that was new, and sweat clung to her face like rain on a windowpane. I sat down by her. I asked no question, but as if I had she said, "Lot of minutes in a day, and you can't skip any. So don't count 'em, stay busy. Better to wonder where the day went than wonder if it'll end." She stared at the garden, not as something she took pleasure in giving her labor to, but as a penance, a begging prayer she knew would not be answered.

When Mr. Harris was in Montgomery, she spent every minute with him and never looked at the garden. But when he was gone, she went out and wrestled there with his fate, knowing it was no use at all. By the end of April she had worked herself almost literally to the bone. During that time Jim was as absorbed in school as I was in the store. But he always had a true instinct about people he cared for. I never heard him ask a bad question, or get mulish and mean the way most children will when they're tired, or for no reason. However he might sometimes kick and bite at me in the brother way, with Hazel and Mr. Harris he was good. Mr. Harris wasn't there on the twenty-seventh, but a few days before, he had taken Jim Downtown and bought him a new suit of clothes, with both short and long pants, for his birthday. Jim was so proud of that, he appeared not to mind the quiet time he and Hazel and I had on his real birthday. Because of my working and Jim's schooling we were seldom home when Mr. Harris came in from a run or left on one, so he and Hazel had their privacy.

When the big *It* finally caught up, it was different from the way I had imagined. That quiet man did a most unquiet thing.

Monday morning the second week of May it was. I went

to work as usual. After the first rush of business, Harvey and I set about getting the store in order, and Mr. Weaver left in his truck for the packing house to buy the day's meat. An hour later he came back with a forequarter of beef and a whole hog, which he had then to cut up. It wasn't until nine-thirty that he opened the *Advertiser* on the back counter where he usually spread it out earlier to read in peace. Almost as soon as he did, he called to me, his voice unlike him, so I hastened to him directly. He pointed at a story on the second page with the headline: *Engineer Killed in Freak Accident.*

There was his name and the place.

George Harris.

New Orleans.

It had happened yesterday in the freight yard after Mr. Harris came in from his run. His fireman had hopped off. (The fireman said later that Mr. Harris pushed him.) Then the disengaged engine had gained sudden speed and crashed head on into a line of boxcars. It had all taken less than a minute.

Mr. Weaver was saying something to me. "Does she get a morning paper?"

"No, sir. Not unless Mr. Harris brings one. She gets the *Journal* delivered in the afternoon."

"You better go to her." He folded the newspaper and handed it to me. "You better take this with you."

Pearl Wigglesworth was on her porch with two women of the neighborhood I recognized. They were exclaiming to each other in heavy whispers; so when they saw me and stopped, I knew they knew. Pearl lifted her fist and spoke directly to me for the first time. "God don't love ugly!" she exulted.

I felt like killing her, but I went into and through

Hazel's house calling her name until I found her in the back yard. When she heard the door slam, she looked over and saw me. Dropping the hoe she'd been using, she looked surprised for only a moment before coming to meet me. "What's that?" Her eyes were on the newspaper. I held it out, folded to the story. She took it from me, but her hands shook so, she couldn't read it. She gave it back to me. "Read for me."

I did.

She didn't say a word, but turned and looked at the garden. Going to it, she picked up the hoe. She swung it rapidly and with awful accuracy, cutting down everything that stood before her. She left no flower, no bud, no live leaf, no upright stalk. She worked as if she would have slain the very earth she stood on if she could. It was only when the destruction of the garden was complete that she began to cry.

"Yesterday!" she said over and over. "A whole day I didn't know!"

I wanted to help her, but she wouldn't let me. She turned and hunched her shoulders every time I went close. When she was quiet, it was not the stillness of peace after storm but the pause between lightning and thunder. In the midst of her next outburst she suddenly became aware of the faces of Pearl Wigglesworth and the two women I'd seen Pearl with earlier peering at her intently over the side fence. She stopped crying, ran for her hoe and threw it with both hands in a wide, angry arc toward the fence. As it clattered harmless to the ground, the women scuttled into the house next door, cackling to each other like so many hens disturbed on the nest.

Hazel was quiet again. I followed her into her house, and she dropped into the kitchen rocker Mr. Harris had so often sat in to watch her prepare a meal. She would sit gator-still for a while and then rock herself violently, her mouth open as if she were screaming, although she made no sound. I fixed us some bologna sandwiches around twelve o'clock, but she wouldn't eat. If I offered her anything or said anything to her, she'd shake her head without saying a word. I finally just sat in one of the straight chairs feeling useless.

At three o'clock Jim came. When he found us in the kitchen, he went straight to Hazel and said, "I'm home. Mrs. Weaver was waiting for me when school let out. She told me and brought me in the truck."

"That was nice of her," Hazel said. She looked at Jim, looked deep at him. "You loved him, didn't you?" she said. Their faces crumpled together. They held each other and cried their hearts out. What I hadn't been able to do for her, Jim did. He gave her the comfort, small but important, of sharing her grief. Later, I was able to get both of them to eat some supper.

I dreaded bedtime, but when it came, Hazel said to me, "You mind if I borrow Jim tonight?" I said no. "You mind?" she said directly to him. He shook his head. "Well then," she said, "let's go to bed. Nobody should have to spend the first night alone."

CHAPTER 28

Mr. White's name suited him. One hunch more and he'd have been an albino, Hazel said. As it was, his eyelids were so pink I couldn't look straight at him the first time I saw him. He was the lawyer Mr. Harris had hired for all the business to do with Hazel's house. He came to see her the day after we read about the accident and was still there when I went home for my noon dinner.

When he left, Hazel told me he'd brought a letter Mr. Harris had written her and mailed to Mr. White to give her "if anything happened." She read it over and over and carried it in a dress pocket for a week before putting it away. The only direct reference to it she made was to say, "He knew all the time. Before he brought me here and did this." She waved her hand to indicate the house, then patted the letter in her pocket. Mr. White explained what she already knew: the house and furnishings were hers, legally done in her name. He also told her that Mr. Harris had made a bank deposit for her of three thousand dollars after Mr. Roosevelt had reopened the banks, and he gave her the bankbook to keep. There was no question of a will, or of anyone's finding out about her and challenging her ownership—there wouldn't be "in such circumstances."

Taking the practical attitude, Hazel was not bad off. Three thousand dollars was a lot of money in those days. So when she said, "What am I going to do?" it had nothing to do with money need, which was the need everybody most feared and talked about during the Depression. She slept in her room alone after the first night, saying as we went to bed the second night, "Got to get used to it sometime, might as well start now." But when doors were closed and lights turned out, I heard her many a night, through the walls and across the hall, saying to herself with a desperate sigh, "Oh me. Oh me."

After first grief the main evidence of how lost she felt was restlessness coupled with a kind of preoccupation that could seem merely absentminded. The look on her face was of someone waiting and listening. I remembered a cow we'd had on the farm whose new calf was sold before being weaned because Papa needed the money. The cow went everywhere looking for the calf. Not finding it, she would lift her head and bawl out a rebuke and a call, until one day she seemed to have forgot all about it.

Of course, Hazel didn't forget. She cleared up the mess of her garden in her back yard, but she didn't plant it again. She would throw herself into sewing for a day or two, making me or herself a dress, or Jim some new nightgowns. She'd cook everything at once she knew Jim especially enjoyed, and then she wouldn't cook anything until it was a mealtime, and open cans or fry something that cooked quick. She wouldn't leave her house and yard unless it was necessary, and then for only the shortest time, hurrying home as if she expected to find a letter or the telephone ringing. She ignored neighbors as deliberately as they had formerly ignored her, they who were so eager now to share her "hard time luck" as they called it to me in the store, where they came to ask how she was, as the next best thing to asking her themselves.

Every day Jim went over his lessons with her and told her what had happened at school. I tried to make ordinary things that had gone on at the store sound lively. Hazel listened, but she didn't care any more. Come night and I'd hear again, "Oh me," through the walls. Come morning and I'd hear Hazel snoring the snorting snore that means exhaustion. I'd get up and go off to work, waking Jim just as I left so he'd get to school on time. And come night again, it was mostly private thoughts and the radio on, with now and then the question, "What am I going to do?"

CHAPTER 29

The last time we saw Hazel in her white uniform was on Wednesday of the final week of school. Mr. Weaver gave me two hours off from the store so Hazel and I could go see Jim in a program in the school auditorium. We sat together at the very back while the children came out and did various things. The funniest was six little girls who came skipping onto the stage in gym bloomers and did some exercises while somebody, the gym teacher it must have been, counted for them out of sight back of the curtain. That got a lot of giggles from the audience, some even from the mothers who had come to see their children perform.

Jim recited a poem called *Who Has Seen the Wind?*
we'd heard him practice at home. He got through it word-
perfect but about twice as fast as we'd ever heard him do it.
There was enough good-natured clapping after it to make
him boastful when he came to find us after the program to
take us to the second grade classroom to meet Miss Kramer
and see the exhibit of art work that covered every wall and
blackboard. Jim had two pieces on display, both done in
crayon and both with gold stars pasted at the bottom by his
name to show they were good. Miss Kramer was a short
woman of no age, dark-complected, almost swarthy. She
had big expressive brown eyes back of square horn-rim
glasses. After she said several times how smart Jim was and
we thanked her, it was time to go. Jim was as glad for us to
go as he'd been insistent on our coming in the first place.

Friday, school was over and Jim got his report card. He
made A's in everything except music and that was a B. At
the bottom it said "Promoted to the Third Grade" in
pretty penmanship and was signed: Flora Kramer. That
night, when I went home from the store, Hazel told us she
had packed her suitcase and was going to take the Greyhound bus to New Orleans for a few days after we had
supper.

"But don't worry, I'll be back. I'm just going down to see
about things."

True to her word she came back the following Wednesday. The only explanation she made was mysterious. "I was
a fool. I looked everywhere, but he wasn't there any more
than he's here."

She seemed to take up her old life, but I could tell she
was restless, unable to resign herself and settle down. She
and Jim went to a picture show now and then, Hazel not
bothering to wear the white uniform. The people at the

Strand and Paramount were used to her, even if they no longer believed Jim had fits.

I was aware that Mrs. Weaver had been keeping her worried eye on us. In fact, when Hazel was in New Orleans she asked me if I wasn't scared to sleep in the house, just Jim and me. I said, "Who's going to bother us?"

"Nobody, I suppose." She fidgeted with her handkerchief, thinking. "Young couple in my back apartment upstairs haven't paid their rent the last two months. It's only ten dollars a month, but they say they haven't got it. I'm thinking of making them move."

I nodded. I knew it was Mrs. Weaver who saw to the tenants in the two apartments upstairs at their house on Mildred Street. Mr. Weaver would have nothing to do with them. In one of the apartments there was a young couple, the wife going to have a baby, the husband doing piecework when he could get it as a house painter. They'd lived there less than six months. An old woman named Mrs. Sarlan lived by herself in the other one. She said her name was Syrian, but she looked like everybody else except for a black wart between her eyes. She liked to complain about the quarrels the young couple was always having.

"What's Hazel going to do?" Mrs. Weaver said.

Surprised at the question, I said, "I don't know."

"She ought to get married to somebody," she said.

I laughed. I couldn't picture Hazel married to anybody at all.

But I thought about it after that, and the more I considered the idea the better it seemed to me. I thought of the lonesome look she so often had, and remembered the cow and calf. Hazel wasn't a cow, and she wasn't lonesome for her calf—she had Jim if that was all she needed. But she needed something, so maybe it was to have her own man. *I* didn't understand that, but everybody's different.

One hot night when she and Jim and I had taken our chairs out to sit in the back yard, where it was a little cooler than indoors, she said her usual, "What am I going to do?" expecting no answer.

But I said to her, "Why don't you get married?"

It was as if I'd thrown a brick through a window. After a minute to get over their shock she and Jim both began to gabble, but Jim soon left off and I began to understand Hazel.

"—me to marry some big dumb bozo and raise a houseful of pickaninnies? Trudy, can you see me doing that? After Mr. Harris? You must have gone crazy with the heat."

"What's so crazy about it?"

"What do I need with a husband? Tell me that. Haven't I got you and Jim for company?"

"Then why aren't you satisfied?"

"Give me time," she said in such a quiet voice I was ashamed of suggesting what I had.

But Hazel didn't become any more satisfied. She wouldn't make friends with neighbors, saying when I urged her to, "Shit on all of them. If they looked down on me because of Mr. Harris, I look down on them because they're shitty."

Jim got a little harum-scarum as the summer went on. I think it was a combination of missing school and knowing Hazel was not as concerned about him as she used to be. Also, he missed Mr. Harris. I didn't. I had respected him, been grateful to him for treating Jim so nice and for letting us stay; and, finally, after he died I had even begun to understand him a little, I think. But I hadn't really cared about him. Jim wasn't mischievous, he just didn't have enough to keep him busy. He played some with the neighbor children, but they never accepted him because he was white and because Hazel wouldn't let them play in her yard.

Things rocked along like that. Of the three of us I was best off because I had my job, and increasingly Wade's friendship, for he worked full time in summer and we got to know each other pretty well. Harvey didn't bother me at all any more. He knew what I thought of him for trying to make trouble for me, so he ignored me as much as he could, which was all I wanted from him.

Along in early August I decided Hazel was up to something. A few times she mentioned having seen Mr. White at his office Downtown. "Just dropped in. Had a little business." But August in Montgomery is not the kind of weather to make people move around much without a car, and everywhere Hazel went it was walk or ride the hot bus. There were more regular letters from New Orleans, which she never had much to say about. Then one day at the store Mrs. Weaver happened to mention that Hazel had been to see her. When I showed surprise, she said, "Maybe I ought not to have said anything yet. I do wish people wouldn't try to make me party to secrets!"

That night I came right out and asked Hazel if something wasn't going on. It seemed to give her the chance she hadn't known how to make for herself.

"Might as well tell you now, though I was going to wait till it was settled. —Jim, put down that book and come over here and listen.

"Well. All this time I been asking myself and asking you what am I to do, and finally it come clear to me. I love you both, but without Mr. Harris this is not the life for me. I thought it was, and Mr. Harris set it all up for me. I've tried it and now I know it's not right for Hazel Fay." She paused, thinking, and Jim and I waited for her to go on. "You got your life ahead, and you're doing fine, both of you. And going to do better when Mr. Roosevelt gets the world straightened out."

Jim grabbed her hand, unable to hold himself any longer. "I want you to stay here!"

She squeezed his hand but then made him let go. "You'll get used to me not being around."

"No!" we both said.

"You're not a baby any more, Jim. You're eight years old, and Trudy is nearly—"

"Don't you say she's nearly fifteen yet!" Jim said. "Because she's not and won't be till nearly next Christmas!"

She laughed a little and slapped him on the thigh. "You might as well get over being jealous of that, because you're never going to catch up with her."

"I want you to stay here," he said stubbornly.

"You telling me you *are* a baby still? After all we been through together?" She winked at me. "Trudy, you and me have been wrong about this boy. We thought he was smart and growing up fast, but he tells me he's not. We better start calling him 'Orphan Jim' again!"

"Don't you dare!" he shouted, glaring at both of us. "Don't either one of you dare, you hear me?"

"Well then," she said as if that settled it.

I said, "Are you going back to the House down in New Orleans?"

"No. That's what I haven't had a chance to tell you yet. You see, when I was down there early this summer, one of the girls I always got along with named Annie-Bell got to going to try it when she'd saved a little more money. After talking how she'd like to have her own House and was I come home, I studied about it and wrote to her and suggested we do it together. I had the money and she was down there to do all the getting things ready.

"Mr. White is going to see about selling this house for me. I've told him no hurry, wait till he can get a good price, because I got cash in the bank. You-all were to stay here as long as you wanted. But the more I thought that over, I saw it wouldn't work." She looked at me. "So I paid another visit to Mrs. Weaver. You remember you told me about those people in her back apartment hadn't paid the rent?" I nodded. "Idea come to me, and it turned out to be in her head too." She smiled. "I think it's all part of how upset she was, having to tell a lie about Jim living there to the lady come from the Board of Education. The way she sees it, if you both move there, it'll make truth of the lie! She's a funny woman, but not so bad. She's already told that couple they got to leave, pregnant be damn.

"Back apartment is two rooms, big enough, and you can take anything you want from here to furnish, because what you don't take I'm going to sell. Mrs. Weaver wants Jim to help her some around the house. Says she misses having a boy to help her since Wade got big and turned to working at the store. She's going to let you have the rooms and your victuals for twenty dollars a month. That's fair; we worked it out together. And with you she's sure of getting her rent. You'll have to share the bathroom with that Mrs. Sarlan, but old people don't go to the bathroom much, that or they go all the time, and Mrs. Weaver says she don't."

We sat quiet for a long time, until Jim said, "How come you want to leave us, Hazel?"

"I don't, Jim, but you and Trudy got to make your life, so I better make mine again, not depend on you and Trudy the way I come to depend on Mr. Harris. I hate to be by myself. I got used to having a lot of people around me. With a House down there of my own, there will always be the girls, you understand? The lights will never all go out at the same time unless there's a hurricane. If I stayed here, I might take to drinking—oh yes. And some Saturday night when I was feeling sorry for myself and you were both off somewhere, as you'd surely be when you got older, I'd go to the kitchen and cut my throat." She laughed and reached over to knuckle his head. "I want you always to be able to think of Hazel in her own House with a lot of pretty girls around, and all the lights on, and the sports making free with their money, and everybody having a good time."

One night just before school started in September we found ourselves at the bus station watching Hazel leave. What we said to each other was nothing special; it never is at such times. What we felt is not to be told as Hazel waved from one of the back windows of the Greyhound bus.

We walked down the block to Montgomery Street to get the city bus that would take us to Mrs. Weaver's house on Mildred Street. We'd already moved our things in. As we waited on the corner I thought of other times we'd parted from people. Jim must have been thinking along the same line, because just as the bus stopped to pick us up he said, "Why do I have to lose everybody but you?"

"Because you're an orphan!" I hollered at him.

CHAPTER 30

It didn't finish there, but other things started that are no part of what I set out to tell. I'm not a woman has to tell everything she knows. We got through the Depression the way everybody else did: working and doing without, having colds and going to movies. We lived on lists. When I think of the Depression, I think of lists. We wrote down things we had to have. We made lists of what we wanted when we could afford it. We listed dates on which or by which time certain things must come, should come, or, please God, would come.

The big grip schooling held on Jim continued and if anything increased, some of it rubbing off on me. After Hazel left, Jim and I shared his lessons. I learned much of what he learned. Then at Wade's urging I took night courses in Bookkeeping and Business English, and in 1937 got a job as assistant office manager in a pickle factory in North Montgomery. The pay was good, but I missed Day Street. When Dr. Hoskins headed the night-time Extension courses for the University of Alabama at Baldwin Junior High School, I went to see him and he let me sit in on some of the courses. He took an interest in me and later in Jim.

Jim finished Lanier Senior High School in 1942 and joined the Navy. When the War was over, he had made up his mind to study for the ministry. I don't think it had anything to do with the War, but maybe I'm wrong. I never asked how he had come to it. By then we were too close ever to ask each other a truly personal question. Dr. Hoskins offered advice and encouragement, and Jim had government help because of his war service. I was never taken with religion the way it takes some people, and I hadn't paid much attention to Jim's going to church as a boy. It was more social than religious, I always thought. Most people went to church then.

Jim told me that many a time when he was off at the Seminary a ten- or twenty-dollar bill would come in the mail and he'd know it was from Hazel, even though it was usually folded in a blank sheet of paper. No use pulling a long face about prostitution paying for the Lord's work. When hasn't it?

During his training he preached sermons in little churches that had no permanent minister of their own. But when as a kind of graduation gift Dr. Hoskins arranged for

Jim to preach a sermon in one of the big churches in Montgomery, that was special. All his friends planned to go hear him. I wrote Hazel and she wrote back excited, saying she wanted to come and hear him too. She asked if she should bring a white uniform. It was before the days of the Supreme Court decision on segregation, before Martin Luther King's activities in Montgomery. I talked to Dr. Hoskins, and he made it all right. In fact, he was at the door when she and I got there together and saw that we were ushered down to the front row.

Although we'd been in touch by letter, I hadn't seen Hazel since that hot September night she waved good-by to us from the bus and headed down to New Orleans. She'd always had good clothes. She wore Navy blue with white collar and cuffs and a hat made entirely of flowers. After the service and handshaking we took her back to my apartment for noon dinner. I'd done everything ahead of time, but I had to go to the kitchen to get it ready to serve. Jim poured a celebration drink for us. As we touched glasses, I said, "What was all the laughing when I was in the kitchen?"

Hazel said, "Jim was telling me one of the most frequent comments he gets is, 'Oh, Reverend, you just can't know how a real sinner feels.' So I gave him his answer. He's to tell them he's a sinner himself, because he slept with a whore when he was only eight years old."

I didn't marry until 1952, when I was nearly thirty-four. Wade and his wife had called me an old maid for ten years. Jim spoke the ceremony. I hate ceremonies. The happy ones are never quite happy; they so often parody what they seek to honor. As Jim spoke the solemn words, it seemed to me for a moment that we were children again, but looked at each other with the sweet mockery of long memory. Then, giving my hand to the man beside me, I heard the voice I sometimes hear in dreams without at first recognizing it as my own.

Good-by, Orphan Jim.